SUN SHINE
& SHADOWS

K.C. WELLS

Sunshine & Shadows
Copyright © 2020 by K.C. Wells
Cover Art by Meredith Russell
ISBN: 978-1-915861-80-1

Chapter One

September
What do they say? You can never go back?

Unfortunately, as far as Horn Pond was concerned, they were right. Stephen Taylor stood by his car in the parking lot off Lake Avenue, trying to block out the traffic's roar along Arlington Road.

God, it's far worse than it was when we were kids. Was it always this noisy?

The thought of him and Jamie crossing the busy road with cars hurtling themselves along it had always given their moms heart attacks—so they claimed— but that was all part of the adventure back then. Stephen wasn't so sure he'd be happy doing it now. The last time he'd visited Horn Pond, he'd been thirteen and miserable. Even Jamie had been down, and that wasn't like him. Of course, that might have had something to do with the fact that they were about to be separated by the entire continental US.

Stephen smiled to himself. It had been a while since he'd thought about Jamie Lithgow. Which was kind of sad, considering how inseparable they'd been as kids. Hell, they practically lived in each other's houses, and it had been like that since they were six. Neither of them had brothers, only a sister each, and maybe that was why they'd been so close. They might have gone through their whole lives like that if it hadn't been for his dad's transfer.

I wonder where Jamie is now? Thirteen years

had flown by since they'd both lived on Ravine Road in Winchester, north of downtown Boston. For all Stephen knew, Jamie could still be living there, although he doubted it. He'd have gone to college, then probably found himself a wife and settled down someplace. *Hey, he could have kids of his own by now.* When Stephen learned his dad was starting his own accounting company back in Boston, the thought had flitted through his mind to look Jamie up. He was curious to know how 'the boy with the laughing eyes' as his grandma called Jamie, had turned out.

He still wasn't sure if he was going to follow through on that, with no real idea why he should be reluctant. Then he realized his initial thought on arrival at the pond had been accurate.

You can never go back.

That might be true, but that didn't mean Stephen wasn't going to indulge in a little reminiscing.

He gazed at his surroundings, relieved to see the boat launch was still there, as was the pumping station. And out on the calm waters of the pond, swans floated serenely by, accompanied by an occasional flurry of ducks.

Damn. I forgot to bring something to feed the ducks.

Then he smiled again. The pond wasn't going anywhere, and provided Dad didn't keep Stephen's nose to the grindstone, there would be other occasions to feed the wildlife.

He hoped. Dad was awfully fired up about the new business, and Stephen suspected there was a great deal of work on the horizon. Work was fine, though. It kept his mind off… other things.

He strolled over to the lake, standing there for a moment to gaze out over the expanse of still water. Where the sunlight hit, it was so bright it made his eyes water, even with his sunglasses in place. As for which way to go, that was easy—the path off to the left, away from Arlington Road.

Stephen recalled the many times he and Jamie had raced along the path that clung to the edges of the lake, winding beneath the trees, its surface mostly paved but with a few trickier places farther along. At least that hadn't changed. The foliage was a little denser, but the dappled shade the canopy provided was very pleasant. Fall colors were already beginning to show themselves, and the sight brought an unexpected lightness to him. Fall had to be his favorite season.

Jamie had been the one to most appreciate the natural beauty of the place: all Stephen had seen were trees and water. But then, Jamie had always been the more creative and artistic one. *He's probably an interior designer now, or an artist, or some other career that's equally aesthetic.* Maybe it was something about growing older, even though twenty-six could hardly be classed as old: Stephen appreciated the pond's beauty more than he'd ever done as a kid.

He walked slowly along the path, knowing exactly where it would lead—Lion Park, where a narrower path looped around a pear-shaped clearing with its benches at intervals, facing inward toward a lawn, and the statue of a lion lay hidden in the center of a clump of trees. He vividly recalled Jamie turning up with a plastic sword one day, because he'd wanted to pretend he was Peter from The Lion, The Witch, and the Wardrobe. They'd climbed onto the lion's back, and yelled things like, "Over there, Aslan! Get the witch! Bite her in the ass!"

If that lion would've moved, we'd have both shit a brick. And if their moms had heard them say the word shit, they wouldn't have been able to sit down for a week.

When he reached the clearing, Stephen sighed. Some of the trees surrounding the lion had been chopped down, leaving it open on one side. *It was better behind the trees*, he thought sadly. They'd pretend it was crouched, poised to pounce on unaware passers-by. In his head he could still see Jamie creeping toward the trees, wearing the grin that never seemed to leave him for long.

Lord, my head is full of Jamie today.

Not surprising really. The visit had opened up the floodgates, and his memories tumbled free, crashing over him in a torrent. Stephen had loved his life in Boston, and the first six months after they moved to California had been the harshest. He'd hated his new school, he'd hated the climate, but most of all, he'd hated leaving Jamie.

We should have tried harder to keep in touch.

That raised an internal snort. They'd been *kids*, for God's sake. Adults might have made an effort to maintain contact, but thirteen-year-old boys? There'd been too much going on in Stephen's life, and he had to assume the same was true of Jamie's. The following five years of high school had passed quickly, and although he'd made friends, there had never been anyone like Jamie.

My best friend. No, there'd been no one who'd gotten close to being that in the years since they'd parted. Stephen could still recall the way they'd moaned and complained when his dad had shared the news of his transfer. Another state would have been bad enough, but the distance between Boston and San Diego had been too vast to contemplate. No tears, at least not where anyone could see them—because since when did thirteen-year-old boys cry?—and definitely no hugs, only Stephen sitting in the back of the taxi as they left for the airport, staring through the rear window at Jamie who stood on the sidewalk, waving.

Did he find another best friend? Not that Stephen would have wanted Jamie to be miserable, but he hoped he'd proved a hard act to follow.

Stephen walked over to the statue, noting the figure in front of it in a wheelchair, his back to Stephen. From what Stephen could see, the guy was sketching the lion's head, his artist's pad balanced on the arms of his chair. He seemed lost in his task, and Stephen did his best to approach quietly, curious to see his work but not wishing to disturb him. As he drew closer, the guy gave a start and jerked his head in Stephen's direction.

"I was expecting you to be dressed like a ninja at leas—" The guy's jaw dropped and his eyes widened. "Stephen?"

Holy fuck. It was Jamie. Older, filled out a little more, but definitely Jamie.

"Oh my God." Stephen blinked a couple of times, but it was still Jamie Lithgow sitting there, gazing up at him in obvious astonishment. His hair was the same shock of black it had always been, but his face was leaner than Stephen remembered.

Then Jamie grinned, and the intervening thirteen years fell away. That smile hadn't changed a bit. "Well, what do you know? Stephen Taylor grew into a bean pole. What did they do over there in California—sprinkle you with Miracle-Gro?" His eyes sparkled.

"Fuck you, feather-brain." The often-used insult slipped from his lips without a second's hesitation, and he burst into laughter. "Christ. I haven't said that in a long time."

"You mean you had no one over there on the West coast to bug you like I did? Aww, you poor thing. How you must've suffered." That sparkle hadn't left Jamie's eyes.

Then it sank in. Stephen lowered his gaze and took in the wheelchair. "Why are you in this contraption? And how long have you been in it?" The moment the words left his mouth, Stephen regretted them. "Sorry. That was rude of me."

Jamie gave a shrug. "If you'd said nothing, I'd be thinking 'who is this guy, and why is he wearing a Stephen face mask?' But that's a long story."

"I've got time," Stephen blurted out. He was still reeling from finding Jamie in one of their favorite haunts. Besides, he wasn't about to go anywhere until he knew more about that wheelchair. He stared at Jamie. "I can't believe you're here. I was just thinking about you, remembering when we were kids."

Jamie gave him a thoughtful glance. "Boston King Coffee isn't far from here, and they do a great raspberry and white chocolate muffin. Plus, their cafe mocha is to die for. That's if you want to go someplace and talk."

Stephen nodded. He had about a million questions. He peered at the wheelchair. "Does it fold up? I think I can fit it into my trunk."

Jamie's lips twitched. "Don't worry. It folds up fine. And I'll be getting there in *my* car, thank you very much."

He blinked again. "You drive?" Then he gave himself a mental kicking. He hadn't meant it to come out the way it did.

Jamie chuckled. "Do you see a tailpipe fitted to this thing? Of course I drive. Lemme put this away." He went to close the sketch pad, but Stephen stopped him.

"Can I see?"

"Sure." Jamie handed over the pad, and Stephen gazed at the intricate pencil drawing.

"Wow. You were always artistic, but this… this is amazing." It was like looking at a black and white photograph, it was so realistic.

"Why, thank you." Jamie took the pad from Stephen and closed it, slipping it into a large leather bag on his lap. "Where are you parked? By the boat launch?" When Stephen nodded, Jamie turned the chair around. "Me too. Then let's go. I was gonna go grab a coffee anyway." His hands were covered in fingerless gloves.

"Should… should I push you?" Stephen was at a loss to know how to act.

Jamie arched his eyebrows. "Why would you wanna do that? Unless of course you're nursing this lifelong dream to push a wheelchair. I hate to burst your bubble, but it's not as exciting as you've been led to believe."

Stephen snorted. "Still got that same ol' sense of humor."

"Seriously though, I'm a mean mover in this baby." There was that grin again. "I could probably beat you in a race, beanpole." He glanced at Stephen's legs. "But then again…" He gripped the wheels and moved off, heading for the path that led back to the parking lot.

Stephen walked beside him, trying to collect his thoughts. "So where are you living now?" *And why didn't you tell me?* That last thought was mean. It took two to maintain a friendship, and Stephen had been as bad as Jamie at not keeping in touch. *And how would he have known where to reach me anyway?*

"All questions will be answered over coffee. And you'd better believe I've got about a gazillion of my own. The first one being what you're doing back in Boston. Then we've got thirteen years to catch up on." Jamie laughed. "Man, we could be in that coffee shop till they close."

They fell silent as they went toward the parking lot. Stephen watched Jamie's progress. *What on earth happened to him?* He didn't appear ill, and judging by the way he pulled strongly on the wheels, he clearly had upper body strength. They reached Jamie's red Corvette first, and as he watched Jamie lift and move his legs into the car, then quickly fold the wheelchair, remove the wheels, and place all of it in the space behind the passenger seat, it became obvious this was a habitual action.

Jamie paused, his hand on the door handle. "Why don't you come in my car? I can bring you back here after." There was a wicked glint in his eyes that Stephen knew so well. "I promise not to drive *too* fast."

One thing Stephen was sure about in that moment—Jamie Lithgow hadn't changed at all.

K.C. Wells

Chapter Two

Jamie wheeled himself up the ramp and along to the coffee shop's door, Stephen behind him. Jamie was still buzzing. *He's back. Stephen Taylor is* back. Jamie's heartbeat raced, drumming in his chest. *And if I hadn't been by the pond, we might never have met up.*

"Here, let me get the door." Stephen went inside and held it for him. Jamie rolled into the warm interior and sniffed, taking in the scent of coffee and other delights. Behind the counter, Dee waved at him, before coming around to move a chair so he could park himself in his usual spot.

She patted his shoulder. "Your regular order?"

Jamie nodded. "Plus whatever this tall drink of water wants." He felt as though a single blink would be enough to make Stephen disappear again. Then he realized what he'd said. He jerked his head toward Stephen. "Sorry. I shouldn't have come out with that."

Stephen regarded him with obvious surprise. "It's… it's okay." Then he smiled. "You've called me far worse."

Jamie rolled his eyes. "Yes, but I had an excuse then. I was a kid." He was relieved by Stephen's reaction. To Jamie's mind, *tall drink of water* had more than a dash of gay to it, but apparently this had gone over Stephen's head, thank God. *But talk about if the cap fits…*

Jamie put a brake on such thoughts before they

got out of control.

Stephen ordered a latte and the same muffin as Jamie, then took the chair with its back to the wall. Jamie waited until he was seated before easing his wheelchair under the table and applying the brake.

"I guess you come here a lot," Stephen commented, glancing at the shop's interior.

Jamie shrugged. "Only about twice a week for the last five years. Ever since I moved to Woburn."

Stephen became still. "You're not living with your folks?"

Jamie was glad he wasn't drinking. He'd have given Stephen an impromptu coffee shower. "Are you kidding me? What twenty-six-year-old guy in his right mind would want to live with his parents? Talk about cramping my style." Except his style had already been well and truly cramped, and he was sitting in the reason for that. Not that *that* was going to stop him from looking. Somewhere out there was a guy who wouldn't get freaked out by a wheelchair and Jamie's non-functioning legs, and Jamie meant to find him.

Dee walked over with their order, and he gave her a warm smile. "Thanks, hun."

"Anytime, sweetness." Then she was back behind the counter.

"'Sweetness'?" Stephen was smirking. Jamie slid his middle finger up his cheek, like they did when they were kids, and Stephen cracked up. "You haven't grown up, have you?"

"Whereas you apparently haven't finished growing." God, he couldn't believe how tall Stephen was. He had to be six feet. His blue-green eyes remained unchanged, but now Jamie noticed his creamy complexion and firm jaw. *Oh kid, you sure grew up gorgeous. You must've broke hearts in California.* Then he had to smile. "I see you still haven't managed to tame your hair. Still does what it wants, huh?" Stephen's hair stood up on top as it always had done when he was a kid.

Stephen chuckled. "Bastard. I forgot to gel it this morning."

Jamie gave a mock gasp. "I see your potty mouth is still with us." Inside he was as light as air. Jesus, it was like the years of separation had never been.

He sipped his mocha, wincing a little at its heat. "So how long have you been back in Boston?" *And are you staying?*

"A few weeks. I've been helping Mom and Dad with their new house."

Jamie gaped. "They've moved back here? Why? Did they finally get fed up with sunny San Diego? You *do* know how freaking cold Boston gets now? And how much *snow* it gets?" He grinned. "I seem to recall you liked the snow. Wait—what *you* liked was stuffing it down my coat and the back of my jeans."

Stephen held up his hands. "Hey, is it *my* fault you liked wearing baggy jeans? And they've moved back because my dad is starting up his own accounting company. I'm going to be working with him."

It took a moment for his words to fully register, and then Jamie had to contain his joy. Stephen was going to stay in Boston. He fought to maintain a calm exterior, until he realized how much ammunition Stephen had given him. Jamie gave him a look of mock horror. "Oh my God. You're an… accountant."

Stephen glared. "And? What's wrong with accountants?"

"They're a step up from zombies, I guess." Keeping a straight face was an effort.

"Hey!" Stephen narrowed his gaze. "The world needs accountants."

"Of course it does," Jamie affirmed. "Otherwise, it would miss out on so many accountant jokes."

Stephen snorted. "And 4 how many accountant jokes do you know?"

Jamie went into full grin mode. "Trust me, you don't wanna know. But changing the subject—because if we talk accounting for too long, I'll be arrested for being asleep in charge of a wheelchair—are you gonna be living with your parents?"

"For the moment, until I find a place of my own."

Jamie wiped his forehead. "Thank God. You'd go nuts if you had to stay there. Unless your mom has become less of a neat freak in the last thirteen years?"

"Just because she made you take your shoes off when you came into the house did *not* make her a neat freak."

"I agree. I was thinking more about how she used to iron your underwear. And follow the cat around the house with a vacuum cleaner. I swear she almost sucked Fluffy into that thing more than once."

Stephen chuckled. "You remember the cat's name?"

"Hey, that cat loved me," Jamie retorted. "She used to come into your room whenever I was there and curl up in my lap."

"Can I ask about the chair now?" Stephen blurted.

Jamie knew he couldn't avoid the topic—he just didn't want Stephen getting all stressed out and sympathetic. Jamie didn't need anyone's sympathy, not now.

He took a drink from his cup, then pulled off a piece of muffin. When he'd swallowed it, he sighed. "I got hit by a car when I was eighteen, okay? Drunk driver. I sustained an injury to my spinal cord. That's it, end of story." Of course it wasn't, but Stephen didn't need to hear all the details. Hell, even Jamie didn't think about those days anymore.

Stephen became so still. "Eight years ago? Why didn't you contact me?"

Jamie arched his eyebrows. "And of *course*, I had your address because we'd been in constant contact since you left, right?" He was genuinely puzzled. "Besides, why would I? We hadn't heard from you or your parents in a long time. I mean, you'd been gone five years by then. What would have been the point of calling you up—assuming you were at the same address—to tell you I'd had an accident? What would you have done? Got on a plane?" He gave Stephen a smile. "You had your own life to lead."

Stephen swallowed. "Is there... is there any chance you'll walk again?"

Jamie shook his head. "This is me for life now. And it's a good life," he added quickly. "So don't you go thinking I'm struggling, or unhappy, or whatever other negative adjectives creep into your head. I'm happy, Stephen."

That was the truth. Only one thing would make his life perfect, but there was no sign of Mr. Right on the horizon. And until he turned up, Jamie would make do with his toys, and his nights alone on the couch or in his bed.

Stephen fell silent, picking at his muffin. Jamie would have given anything to see inside his head right then. When he couldn't stand the silence any longer, he broke it the only way he knew. "Did you know, there are three types of accountants?"

Stephen raised his chin, his lips twitching. "Oh, really?"

Jamie nodded. "Those who can count, and those who can't." To his relief, Stephen laughed, and he breathed more easily. "What's the most wicked thing a group of young accountants can do?"

"I dread to ask."

Jamie flashed him a grin. "Go into town and gang-audit someone."

Stephen held up his hands. "Please, stop."

"Only if you agree to meet up with me again." There was no way he was going to let Stephen walk out of his life again. Jamie wanted his best friend back.

"You want me to?"

Jamie chuckled. "Are you kidding? It's gonna take at least five more coffee meet-ups for me to get through my repertoire of accountant jokes."

"When you put it like that, how can I refuse?" Stephen took another bite of his muffin, only this time with more enthusiasm.

Jamie had a million questions, but they'd have to wait. Stephen would want to know more about the accident, Jamie was certain of that. Not unless he'd changed beyond recognition: he'd always been inquisitive as a kid.

Has he changed that much? Stephen had been a good-looking boy, but Stephen the adult was far more handsome. *Who am I kidding? He's beautiful.* And yet…

He looked closer. *Is he happy?* Jamie couldn't tell. He hoped Stephen's life in California had been good. Certainly nothing like Jamie's life.

He knew Stephen would find it hard to believe Jamie was genuinely happy, because who could believe a guy in a wheelchair was happy? But he was. He had his independence, parents who supported him, a sister who loved spending time with him… The dark days of the past were far behind him.

And now Stephen's back. Jamie had to fight hard to hide his elation. As soon as the words feather-brain fell from Stephen's lips, Jamie knew his best friend was still in there somewhere. It had always been Stephen's favorite insult for him, not that Jamie had minded one bit.

"Do you live alone?"

Jamie blinked and dropped back into the moment. "Hm? Oh, yeah. I have a place not far from the pond."

"Just you?"

Jamie locked gazes with him. "Yes, just me. And it's been *just me* ever since I moved here." *Unfortunately.*

Stephen said nothing, but continued eating his

muffin.

It didn't take a genius to know what was going through Stephen's mind. Jamie had met plenty of people who seemed to believe having a disability meant having to rely on others.

Well, not in Jamie's book. He could—and did—take care of himself. And he'd make sure Stephen understood that.

"Seeing as you're going to be around, maybe you could come see where I live," he said on an impulse. "I could make us dinner."

Stephen's eyes glittered. "You can cook?"

Now *that* was the Stephen he remembered. "Yes, you asshole."

"Is this the same Jamie who failed his home economics badge at summer camp? The one who set fire to the—"

"I thought we said we'd never talk about that. Ever." Jamie glared at him.

"In that case, I'd love to come for dinner sometime. I'll be sure to have the number handy for the Emergency Room."

Jamie stared at him, then burst out laughing. "Making up for lost time, I see. You've really missed me, haven't you?"

Stephen sighed. "Can I be honest?"

He stilled. "Of course."

Stephen gazed into his latte. "For the first three months I kept asking Dad if we could go back to Boston. For the next three months I missed you like crazy. Then I kind of got used to you not being around." He raised his head and looked Jamie in the eye. "I've thought more about you today than in all the last twelve years put together. The moment I got out of my car at the pond, you were there, like we'd never been away."

Jamie smiled. "Why do you think I go there so often? It's where I remember us best."

"Us."

"Yeah, us. Think we can go back to being us, even though we're not kids anymore?" Jamie hoped so. He could do with a friend. He had plenty of acquaintances, but no one person who really got him, not like Stephen used to do.

But will he get me now?

Only time would tell.

"I think… we have a lot more catching up to do."

Jamie heaved an internal sigh of relief. "I agree."

"Only… not now. I'd better go. I told Mom I wouldn't be gone long. I was only taking a breather from unpacking boxes. It feels like that's all I've been doing since we got here."

"Oh." Jamie did his best to hide his dismay. He pulled his phone from his pockets and hit the Contacts button. "Put yourself in there."

Stephen took it, his thumbs moving over the screen. "I'll have to let you know when I'm free next. It's likely I'm going to be busy over the next few weeks. I only managed today because it's a Saturday." He grinned. "And I had to get away from the damn boxes."

"I work from home, so I'm fairly flexible." Jamie gestured to his body. "Unlike the rest of me. Except that's not strictly true. Everything *moves*, it's just that some parts don't do what my brain tells 'em. It calls, but they don't answer." His eyes twinkled. "Kinda reminds me of a few dates I went on." More than a few, unfortunately, but he wasn't about to share *that*.

"How can you joke like that?" Stephen regarded him earnestly.

Jamie chuckled. "I can joke because I'm the one who gets to live in this body. Okay?"

For a moment Stephen said nothing. At last he nodded. "Okay. I guess." He cocked his head to one side. "What do you do for a living?"

Jamie couldn't resist. "Guess."

Stephen bit his lip. "Painter."

Okay, that was unexpected. "Seriously?"

He gestured to the bag on Jamie's knee. "That drawing is amazing. And you were always so... creative."

"I still am, only I do it with tech. I design websites." When Stephen's eyes widened, Jamie laughed. "What's so surprising about that?"

"You... and technology. You used to hate technology class at school."

Jamie gaped. "I was ten. People do learn things, you know."

"But... you were such a dud!"

"I got better, okay?"

They stared at each other, then both started laughing at the same time. Stephen got out his wallet.

"What are you doing?" Jamie demanded.

"Paying the bill. You got a problem with that?"

"Yeah. I invited you, remember?" Jamie pointed to Stephen's wallet. "Put that away. You can pay next time."

"So there *is* going to be a next time?"

Jamie smiled. "You bet. Now let me pay, then I'll take you back to your car."

"On one condition. You don't break any speed limits this time."

"Did I break 'em getting here?" he challenged, already knowing the answer.

"Er, yes? Did you not *hear* me praying? And uttering 'Jesus!' several times? Not to mention holding onto the oh shit handle from the second you squealed out of the parking lot."

Jamie let out a dramatic sigh. "Okay. I'll drive slower. If you insist." Inside he was buzzing again.

My best friend just walked back into my life. Someone up there obviously liked Jamie. He was glad there would be more meet-ups. He still had a heap of questions.

Probably not half as many as Stephen had about Jamie's life.

K.C. Wells

Chapter Three

Stephen let himself into the house and called out, "I'm home."

From the kitchen, he caught his mom's laugh. "Last thing I heard, house breakers don't have keys so I figured it was you." She poked her head around the door. "So where did you go?"

"I went to Horn Pond." He removed his jacket and dropped it onto the hall chair, until he caught Mom's glare, and hastily hung it up on a hook by the door.

"I'll bet it seems smaller than it did last time you were there. There's coffee in the pot if you're interested." She retreated into the kitchen and Stephen followed her, heading for the coffee. "And I'll bet the traffic is still lethal. Every time you went there as a boy, I swear I kept waiting for a call from the ER to say you'd been hit by a car, trying to cross that damn road."

He smiled to himself. *Damn* was about as far as Mom would venture into 'cuss country' as she called it. Then her reference to car accidents struck home. "You are *not* going to believe who was there."

Mom paused in her task of putting away the clean dishes. "Now, how am I supposed to guess that? Either you spotted someone famous, or it's someone I know too."

He poured coffee into the biggest mug he could

find. "Jamie."

Mom froze in mid action. "Jamie Lithgow?" Her face creased into a smile. "Oh my. He's still living in Boston? Has he changed much? Will he be visiting us? How is he?"

Stephen chuckled. "If you let me get a word in, I'll tell you." He sat at the table, his hands wrapped around his mug. Before he could utter another word, Dad came in through the back door, instantly removing his boots.

Mom had them well trained.

He smiled when he saw Stephen. "Hey, you're back. Marie called. She asked you to call her later."

Stephen grinned. "Aw. She misses me already." His older sister lived in Carmel with her husband and their two kids. It still took some getting used to, having to work out the time back there on the coast.

"Stephen saw Jamie Lithgow at Horn Pond," Mom said with a smile.

Dad's eyes lit up. "Aw, that's great. In that case, I'm surprised to see you back so soon. I'd have thought you two would still be catching up come nightfall."

"I wasn't going to leave you two for long, not when there's still so much to do." The moving van had arrived the day after they'd landed, and Stephen figured they had a few more days of shifting and unpacking to go. Besides, he'd felt… awkward.

Seeing Jamie in that wheelchair…

"So how is he?" Mom demanded. "Does he look the same?"

Dad chuckled. "If he does, there's something wrong."

Mom squinted at him. "You know perfectly well what I mean."

"Actually, there *was* one thing about him that was very different." Stephen took a deep breath, unable to shift the image from his mind. "He's in a wheelchair."

They froze, their mouths open. Mom was the first to break the silence. "Is that a permanent thing?" She touched her parted lips with her fingers, her expression dazed.

He nodded. "He's been like this for eight years. A car accident. Someone else's fault."

"Well, damn." Dad's face fell. "I always liked that boy."

Despite his own sorrow at Jamie's situation, Dad's comment rankled. "He's in a wheelchair, not dying of some terminal disease."

Dad blinked. "Yeah, but… I mean… this must have changed him."

Stephen had to smile. "Not so you'd notice. Anyway, we're going to meet up again. As you said, we still have a lot of catching up to do." He didn't want to talk about Jamie. His joy at seeing his childhood friend was marred by the idea of him living life in a wheelchair.

It just wasn't right. Not Jamie.

"You've got more important things to think about," Dad informed him. "Such as finding a place to live. Have you given the matter some thought?"

Stephen hadn't but he knew that wasn't what Dad wanted to hear. "Yeah, I thought I'd start looking in Jamaica Plain. It's not too far away from work or central Boston, and it's got a nice vibe to it." Not that he'd actually been there—he'd seen photos in passing, and had held onto it as a possible place to throw at Dad if the question arose.

"Vibe?" Mom chuckled. "You sound like you're still living in California."

Dad ignored her. "You ready to put that MBA to good use?"

"If you mean, am I ready to work hard, then yes sir." Stephen knew his dad had a lot riding on this. After years of working for one company, the decision to go it alone had been made with a lot of trepidation, but they'd done their research. Now all they had to do was make it work.

"You know what they say," Mom said as she joined him at the table. "All work and no play."

That was Mom-speak for 'find yourself a boyfriend.' Not that she'd ever come right out and say that. It had been eight years since he'd found the courage to come out to them. His parents had been dismayed at first, but Stephen was pretty sure most of that was due to the issue of grandchildren. They'd come around slowly. Not that he'd helped the situation become any more comfortable, what with his string of failed relationships.

Marie, bless her, had been his advocate since he'd come out. She'd been the one who'd consoled him when he got dumped or cheated on. She'd even gone so far as to take him to a gay bar in West Hollywood, determined that she could pick out a better candidate than the ones Stephen had been choosing. It had been a hilarious weekend, but Mr. Right had been away at the time, apparently.

Dad huffed. "That can wait. Right now is for

focusing on building the company. He's got plenty of time for relationships when we're established." He met Stephen's gaze. "And your love life has a habit of taking away your focus. I remember what you were like in college. You were—"

"I know, I know," Stephen interjected. He was in no mood to rehash all his past failings. He pulled his phone from his pocket and stood. "You know what? I think I'll call Marie back now." And without waiting for either of them to say anything, he went out the back door and into the yard.

The late afternoon sun was pleasant on his face, and he went to the bench that sat against the rear fence. Marie answered within three rings.

"Okay, what's happened?"

He laughed. "What makes you think something has happened?"

"Since when do you call me back so promptly? I'm guessing you need to talk." A pause. "You having second thoughts? About working with Dad, I mean? I *do* know what he's like."

"No, it's not that. I got caught up in the middle of Mom hinting I should find someone, and Dad telling me romance will have to wait."

"Did she actually come out with the word boyfriend?"

He snorted. "Coming back to Boston hasn't brought about *that* much of a change."

She heaved a dramatic sigh. "It's your own fault."

"How do you work that out?"

"You couldn't have lied and said you were bi, huh? You know, to lessen the blow?"

Stephen laughed. "No. Because you *know* what would have happened. They'd be forever waiting for me to switch teams." Time to change the subject. "I went to Horn Pond today."

"Aw, that's good." He couldn't miss the genuine note of happiness. "Has it changed much?"

"Not really. But when I was there, I met Jamie."

Another pause. "No freaking *way*. Of all the people…" Quickly he told her about Jamie's situation, and her breathing hitched. "Jesus."

"What really got me? Apart from the wheelchair, he sounds like the old, happy-go-lucky Jamie I remembered. If you heard him, you'd never know what his life is like now."

"Hmm."

He stilled. "What does that mean?"

"It means I don't buy it. I think it was an act for your sake. Think about it. He's not going to tell you a tale of woe, is he? He's putting a brave face on it, because it was you."

That made him stop and think. "You think?" That made his heart ache. Jamie going through hell, and not wanting to share it… For a moment, his throat seized and he couldn't speak.

"Are you okay?" Marie's voice was soft.

Stephen pulled himself together. "Why would I not be okay?"

"Because that business with Carl stressed you out. Three weeks after that bastard walked out, you were still a mess."

"Leave it." Carl was the last person Stephen wanted to think about right then.

"You know where I am if you want to talk."

"What's there to talk about? Apart from the fact that I have lousy taste in men."

"How does the saying go? 'You have to kiss a lot of frogs before you find your prince.'"

He snorted again. "I think I've moved away from frogs and into the toad population."

"You gotta have faith, kiddo. He's out there somewhere. Who knows, maybe what you needed to do was move back to Boston to find him. He might have been waiting there for you the whole time."

God, he loved Marie. "Have I told you recently how wonderful you are?"

"I could use hearing it a few more times." A plaintive wail broke out in the background, and she sighed. "And that's my cue to go see what Natasha has done to her little brother now."

He laughed. "You love being a mom. Don't bother denying it. I'm surprised you stopped at two." When she fell silent, the skin on his arm erupted into goosebumps. "Sis?"

"I wasn't going to tell you yet, because it's early days, and I like having that first scan before I spread the good news, but... I'm pregnant. About seven weeks, I think."

Warmth radiated throughout his body. "Oh, that's awesome. Is Greg happy?"

She laughed. "Greg is turning cartwheels. He wants another boy."

"Was this planned?"

"Not exactly. Let's call it a happy surprise. I've told him no more though. I'm thirty-two, for Christ's sake."

"I won't tell Mom. You can do that when you're

ready."

"Thanks, bro. It'll be a few weeks yet. And in the meantime, you're gonna be a busy boy." She paused. "And I am really sorry to hear about Jamie. He was such a bright, sunny kid. He doesn't deserve this."

Stephen wasn't about to repeat Jamie's insistence that he was happy. He didn't think Marie would believe him. And now she'd put that seed of doubt in his mind, Stephen wasn't sure he believed it either. Maybe he'd feel better once he and Jamie had talked some more.

Because Stephen wanted to believe Jamie.

Chapter Four

Jamie had barely opened his eyes that Sunday morning when his phone sprang into life. He didn't even need to look at the screen to know who it was. Only his mom called this early. He reached for the phone on the nightstand.

"It's a good thing I love you," he joked as he answered the call.

Mom chuckled. "I knew you'd be awake."

"Only just." It had taken him a while to fall asleep, which wasn't like him. And when sleep finally came, it brought dreams of Stephen. Well, him *and* Stephen as kids, playing, laughing...

"I was checking you're still coming for lunch today."

"Sure I am. As if I'd miss your Sunday pot roast." His mom's gravy was a food group on its own. "Is Liz coming?"

"Yes, and that's really why I'm calling you." A pause. "She's bringing someone."

"Way to go, Liz." His sister had been in an abusive relationship, one from which she'd finally broken free the previous year, but there'd been no one on the horizon since then. "What do we know about him?"

"They've been dating about four months. She says he works in her office, and he's really sweet."

Jamie would take a sweet guy any day. "Does

Mr. Sweet have a name? Because I *can* call him that if he doesn't."

Another pause. "Jamie, don't."

"Don't what?" He feigned ignorance, unable to stop himself from smiling.

"I know what you're like when you're in full... Jamie-mode. The poor guy would never recover. Worse, he might never come back."

"You mean, you don't want me to dazzle him with my shining wit and sparkling personality?" He loved yanking her chain.

"Just... tone it down, for this first meeting? It's taken Liz this long to work up to bringing him to meet us. You don't want to scare him off, do you?"

He sighed. "As if I'd do that. I'll behave, I promise."

Her voice softened. "Be my usual sunshine Jamie, and he'll love you." Jamie heard the catch in her breath, and he knew exactly what had passed through her mind.

"There's gotta be someone out there, Mom. Someone made just for me. I have to be patient, that's all." Then he remembered his news. "I went to Horn Pond yesterday."

"Really? Imagine that."

He chuckled. "Dad's right. You can't do sarcasm. But I'm telling you because someone turned up there. Someone you will remember very well."

"Stop teasing and tell me. Who?"

"Stephen Taylor."

This time he was greeted with a gasp. "You're kidding."

"Nope. He's back in Boston, and he's going to

work in his dad's company. But Mom... prepare yourself for a shock."

"What? What's happened to him?"

Jamie fought hard to suppress his laughter. "He's become... an accountant."

There was a second or two of silence before his mom burst into laughter. "You are such a little shit, do you know that? You really had me going there. So... how is he? Has he changed much?"

"Oh my God, he got *tall*. We're talking six feet, minimum. I mean, I know everyone looks tall when I'm in the chair, but *Christ*, Mom."

"How did he take it?"

He knew what *that* meant. "Like you'd expect." Only, Jamie was hoping Stephen would get over the shock fast. He was also praying that shock didn't morph into sympathy. Jamie wasn't sure he could take that from Stephen.

"Is he going to stay in touch?"

"I assume so. We're meeting up again for coffee sometime."

"You got your brother back." Her voice was warm.

Yeah, Stephen had been that, all right. Jamie hoped the past thirteen years hadn't changed him too much. The one memory that stood out was their laughter. God, Jamie had peed himself on more than one occasion when Stephen had regaled him with tales from home. Stephen's mom was a hoot.

"I think he needs to get used to me first."

"Are you going to bring him here one Sunday? We'd love to see him again."

Jamie laughed. "You think he'd say no to that?

He loved your cooking." He glanced at the clock. "Okay. I've got things to do before I see you, so let me get on with them, and I'll be there by twelve."

"Okay. See you soon." Mom hung up.

Jamie put his phone aside, ready to begin his rituals. They were all second nature by now, and he'd been doing them long enough that he could go through his routine on autopilot.

He reached into the nightstand drawer for the make-up mirror and flashlight. Once he'd flipped the mirror onto the magnified side, he threw back the sheets and rolled, his ass facing the mirror. Every morning began the same way, checking for sores or redness. If there was any of the latter, he'd press his fingers into it to make sure the skin blanched. Then he'd roll onto his other side and check again.

Once that was done, it was bathroom time. Jamie lifted his legs out of the bed, then transferred himself into his chair. The first occasion he'd done this, he'd neglected to apply the brakes, and that had been a mess. Thankfully, he'd done it in the hospital during rehab, and it was a lesson he'd never forgotten.

He wheeled himself into the bathroom, stopped his chair next to the toilet, dropped the handle on the elevated commode, and hoisted himself across onto it. When he'd first had the accident, the nurses had gotten him into a routine of emptying his bowels in the evening, but once he was in his own place, he'd changed that. He preferred to get it out of the way first thing.

Then it was shower time. He put the chair next to the tub with its padded transfer bench that sat on the edge. He heaved himself onto it, then maneuvered

onto the seat in the shower. The massager hung down, ready for him, and he cleaned himself. When he was done, he dried himself off as thoroughly as he could, then folded the towel and placed it in the wheelchair. Another transfer, and he
dried off some more. Then it was back into the bedroom to dress.

His closet was organized with all the racks and shelves within reach, and he chose a shirt and sweats. His parents didn't even bat an eye when he turned up wearing those: they knew by now sweats were easier to get in and out of. Of course, getting into them was a matter of rolling from side to side, inching them up over his hips and ass, working it until they were in place, but Jamie was used to it.

Once he was clothed, Jamie made his bed, wheeling himself around it until the comforter was smooth and the pillows were plumped. Then he headed for the kitchen to prepare breakfast.

As he ate his cereal, Jamie's mind went to Stephen. He'd had so many questions, but he could tell Stephen wasn't up to answering them. When he'd said he had to go, Jamie hadn't been surprised. Part of him thought Stephen was fleeing because he couldn't deal with the situation, but he could be wrong.

He *hoped* he was wrong.

Jamie couldn't get over Stephen's appearance. Okay, he'd been a good-looking kid, but *Hoo boy…* Now he was someone to swoon over.

Is it too much to hope he's gay?

Jamie was all for the power of positive thought.

Jamie wheeled himself up the slight incline to his parents' front door. Dad had had the ramp built as soon as Jamie had become mobile. Before he could ring the doorbell, Mom opened it.

"Hi there. Go on through." She stood aside to let him in, and he rolled over the hardwood floor and into the living room. Dad was sitting in his chair, talking animatedly with a young man. It was only then Jamie realized Mom hadn't told him Mr. Sweet's name.

He bit his lip. *Oh, the temptation…*

Dad looked up and smiled. "Hey, you. Good to see you. This is Phil. He works with Liz."

Phil had obviously been warned because he didn't focus on the wheelchair. He got to his feet before Jamie could stop him, and held out his hand. "Pleased to meet you, Jamie. Liz has told me so much about you."

"It's lies, all of it," Jamie blurted out, grinning. "Photoshopped, I swear. They'll never be able to prove a thing. And that video was fake."

Phil blinked, then laughed. "Yeah, she told me about your sense of humor too."

Liz came into the room. "Oh dear Lord, has Jamie started already?" She came over to him and kissed him on the cheek. "Play nice," she warned, her eyes glinting.

Jamie widened his eyes. "Me?" He wasn't surprised when Liz and Dad laughed at that. Phil seemed amused. Jamie sniffed, then let out a groan. "That smells amazing." His stomach rumbled as if in agreement.

Dad chuckled. "Be warned, Phil. Get some mashed potatoes on your plate when you get the chance. *Someone* here is likely to hog them all."

Phil sat, and Jamie moved the chair into the space next to the couch. He speared Phil with an intense gaze. "So, Phil… how long have you been dating my sister?"

Phil wiped his brow dramatically. "Wow. I wasn't expecting the third degree," he joked, but the scrape of his hand through his hair said plenty, along with the way his other hand fidgeted. Liz sat beside him, covering it with hers.

Jamie smiled. "Let me start again. I'm really happy to meet you, Phil. How long have you and Liz been together?"

Phil relaxed visibly. "About four months. She decided it was time I met all of you." His eyes sparkled. "Especially you."

Jamie preened. "Yeah, well, what can I say? I'm special."

Liz chuckled. "Oh, you're definitely that. How's work going? Still got plenty coming in?"

He nodded. "As long as I can find time to go sketching, I'm happy." Working for himself was perfect, and his results brought him more clients. He had to smile at Stephen's remark about Jamie's IT skills. Stephen wasn't wrong. Jamie had sucked in IT class, and it wasn't until he got to tenth grade that it all fell into place. Once he was out of rehab and trying to build his life back up, a course in IT had seemed the obvious choice, especially when he was able to complete it online.

"Did Mom tell you who I ran into yesterday? Not literally, of course."

Dad cackled. "I'm not so sure about that. I've seen you really move in that thing." It was the kind of comment Jamie didn't mind at all.

Liz nodded, her eyes bright. "When are we gonna see him?"

"You mean, so you can rag on him again? He always said you were worse than his own sister." He and Stephen had spent a lot of time in each other's homes when they were growing up, and their parents had socialized too, at parties, birthdays, and the holidays. Jamie snickered. "You wanna watch it though. Stephen grew. And I mean *grew*."

"Then he needs to come here so we can catch up," Mom said as she walked into the living room. "I want to know all about his life in California."

"I already know he's nuts," Liz said with a grin. "Who would leave all that sunshine to come back here?"

"Maybe he missed Jamie," Phil suggested.

Jamie snorted. "I'm pretty certain I didn't feature in his plans." But he couldn't deny it was a pleasant thought.

"Well, if you're all going to stay in here and reminisce, I'll eat the pot roast myself," Mom declared.

Jamie propelled himself toward the door, swerving to avoid a collision with his mom. "Mashed potatoes here I come." The others were right behind him, laughing.

Jamie loved his Sundays. It was good to be someplace where no one underestimated him, no one told him he couldn't do something he'd set his mind to, and no one made negative references to his chair.

He hoped Phil was going to fall in with the rest of them, because thus far, he seemed like a nice guy. Heaven knew Liz needed one of those after the last bastard. Jamie couldn't wait for the day when *he* would bring someone to meet his family.

He needed a nice guy too.

"I've been thinking about going on vacation," Jamie said as Liz collected the dishes, and Mom brought in the dessert, one of her apple pies, with whipped cream.

Dad gave him a quizzical glance. "Next summer?"

Jamie shook his head. "I was thinking more about this winter. I had an idea, something I wanted to try."

"Well, it's obviously not skiing," Phil quipped, but that was as far as he got before Liz fired him a warning look. Mom and Dad fell silent, their gazes flickering in Jamie's direction.

He knew what that meant. *Play nice.* They clearly liked Phil. Well, so did Jamie, but that didn't mean he was going to let Phil think such remarks would be acceptable.

Jamie arched his eyebrows. "Why not?" he

asked in a quiet voice.

Phil blinked. "Well…"

Dad chuckled. "If Jamie wants to go skiing, believe me, he'll find a way. You'd better learn that now."

God bless my dad. He was never one to underestimate Jamie.

Mom peered at him. "I take it there are places where you can?"

He nodded. "There's a place in Vermont where they do adaptive skiing. They give you training first, and you can hire mono-skis, with either twin or one single ski. I've been thinking about it for a while." Jamie was always on the lookout for a new challenge, and he'd never gotten the chance to ski when he was younger. This seemed like the perfect solution.

"I'm sorry," Phil said quickly. "I made an assumption, didn't I?"

Jamie gave him a warm smile. "We all do that, from time to time."

"Yeah, but I won't be doing it again," Phil assured him. "Least ways, not where you're concerned." He cocked his head to one side. "You ever thought about paragliding?"

Jamie caught his breath. "*Now* you're talking. That would be awesome." He had no idea if the sport catered for paraplegics, but he was going to find out.

"It's something I've always wanted to try," Phil told him. "So if you ever decide you want to, I'll do it with you."

Okay, Jamie was sold. He glanced at Liz. "This one's a keeper."

She laughed. "Thanks for the vote, but I'd

already worked that one out for myself."

Phil reached across the table and took Liz's hand in his.

This was going down in Jamie's diary as a good day.

What would make it perfect would be if he had someone else to participate with him. Someone who cared for him. Someone who wouldn't bat an eye at the idea of Jamie hurtling himself down a mountainside on a mono-ski.

Yet another thing to add to Jamie's list of all the things he wanted in a boyfriend.

Chapter Five

Jamie waited for three days for Stephen to get in touch, but by the time Wednesday arrived and no text or call, a little unease began to seep into his usually positive thoughts.

It's the chair, isn't it? It wouldn't be the first time that goddamn chair had gotten in the way. Either guys thought sitting in it somehow dropped Jamie's IQ by several feet, or they thought he was good looking enough to warrant a pity fuck, or even, God forbid, they wished to indulge in some kind of 'cripple kink'—there were some sick fuckers out there. Maybe most of the time what got them going was nothing more than curiosity, until the moment came to actually do the deed, and then they ran a mile.

Jamie hoped every fucking time that he'd done enough to give a prospective bed partner the confidence to ask him anything. He had this whole conversation mapped out in his head—he called it The Talk—but so far that was where it had stayed. That chunk of metal put guys off way before they'd gotten close enough to remove their clothes. What saddened Jamie most—when he let himself think about it, which wasn't often—was that no guy had seen him naked since he was seventeen, and that had been his first time. Frantic fumblings on a school field trip in his senior year were all he had to remember, and they hadn't exactly been magnificent.

Hey, at least I got laid once, right? To Jamie's

way of thinking, being paraplegic *and* a virgin was an infinitely worst-case scenario.

He loaded his dishes into the dishwasher and then grabbed his phone. *You know what they say…* He scrolled through to find Stephen's number. After three or four rings, the call connected.

"Hey, Mohammed. This is the mountain here. Just checking to see when you're planning on paying me a visit."

Stephen chuckled. "Subtle, Jamie. Did you miss me already?"

"Like a hole in the head, bean pole." Just hearing Stephen's voice made him feel good. "So…. Think you could manage dinner tomorrow night? My place?"

"That depends on what you were planning to cook."

Jamie snickered. "I was thinking liver, cauliflower, Brussels sprouts, olives, anchovies. On a pizza."

Violent retching sounds filled Jamie's ears. "You little fuck. I think you just named every single food that makes me heave. Your memory sure hasn't changed."

Jamie buffed his fingernails on his shirt. "Ha. I still got it. Seriously though… is that doable?"

"Sure. What are you drinking these days? Do I bring beer, wine… sherry?"

That last one made him laugh. "Oh my God. You remembered. That Christmas at your grandma's house."

"Hard to forget you decorating her best rug with your own Technicolor yawn."

Jamie gaped. "My own what?"

Stephen rolled his eyes. "You threw up on it, remember? And that's a phrase I learned from an Australian student I met at college"

Jamie also remembered the shame he'd felt the next time he'd seen her. Stephen's grandma was an amazing lady, and he hated to think he'd disgraced himself. And like the lady she was, she'd been sweet about it. She'd also hidden the sherry bottle.

"In answer to your question, I like both beer and white wine, but don't put yourself out on my account."

"Great. I'll see what I can lay my hands on." A pause. "You're not going to give me any clues as to what's on the menu?"

"Aw, come on. Lemme keep *some* air of mystery."

Stephen cackled. "You do know when you say that, I'm picturing you in these floaty veils, and you're holding one across your face, so I can only see your eyes. And you're batting your eyelashes."

"Veils, huh? Well, now we have it. Stephen Taylor grew up kinky." Jamie fucking *loved* this back-and-forth.

"Kinky my ass."

"Hey, if you say so. What you choose to do in the privacy of your bedroom is entirely your affair. Okay… how does seven o'clock sound?"

"I can make seven."

"Great. I'll text you the address. There's a parking space in front of the garage. See you then." Jamie disconnected, his heart light. *He's coming.* Then he headed for the freezer to decide on what to cook.

He was still toying with the idea of liver, for shits and giggles.

Right on the dot of seven, Jamie caught the sound of a car pulling up outside. He rolled toward the front door and opened it as Stephen was locking the car. Jamie chuckled. "I didn't see which car you got into back at the pond, but if I could have picked a car for you? It'd be a Toyota Camry. Definitely an accountant's car."

Stephen arched his eyebrows. "This is what I have to look forward to all evening? More digs? And this is a rental, feather-brain." In one hand he held a brown paper bag. That raised another chuckle.

"It's okay, you don't need to hide the booze. The liquor store stops here daily." Jamie rolled backwards to let Stephen step into the house. "Welcome."

Stephen smiled. "It looks good from the outside." Then he stilled. "That *was* a joke, right? About the liquor store?"

Jamie rolled his eyes. "Lord, what did you do to your brain out there in Cali? Fry it in all that sun?" He held out his hand for the bag, and Stephen handed it over. Jamie peered inside, and his chest tightened. "Oh you sweet man." Next to the bottle of white wine were four packets of Reese's Peanut Butter Cups. Jamie jerked his head up. "You remembered."

Stephen grinned. "So much for the Cali sun frying my brain. Of course, I *could* take them home with me."

"Don't you fucking dare."

Stephen burst out laughing. "I was wondering how long it would be before that mouth of yours let loose."

"*My* mouth? Which of us used the word fuck within ten seconds of meeting up for the first time in thirteen years? Hmm?" Jamie gestured to the hallway. "I'll give you the grand tour. Follow me, but not too close. These wheels take no prisoners, so please keep your hands inside the car at all times."

"I like the floors."

Jamie chuckled. "There are no carpets here. Carpets and wheelchairs do *not* add up to maneuverability." He pointed to a door on the left. "Bathroom. There's a commode but you can lift it out of the way if you need to. Just be sure to put it back when you're done. And you can hang that by the door." He waited while Stephen removed the long black coat. "That suits you, by the way. But then black always did." He grinned. "You had this whole goth thing going on when you were twelve, remember? Well, you tried, but your mom had a fit about it. Something about deathrock being Satan's music?"

"I listened to that crap for all of one week!" Stephen retorted. "It was hardly a 'thing'. And *you* had your moments too, or have you conveniently forgotten those?"

"I forget nothing. It's a curse." Jamie went into the kitchen, Stephen behind him. He pointed to the cabinet next to the refrigerator. "Glasses in there.

Corkscrew in the drawer next to the stove. That's if we need one. You might have splurged and gone for a screw cap."

"Fuck you."

Jamie felt like he was thirteen years old all over again. The first time he'd said the word fuck was in Stephen's presence, and he'd felt so goddamn brave. Of course, then it became commonplace, except when they were around their parents. They'd slipped up a couple times, but the results had been enough to make them more careful.

Stephen sniffed the air. "Something smells good," he said as he reached into the cabinet for the glasses. He pointed to the sink. "I like that."

Jamie knew he was referring to the gap beneath the sink. It made it easier to fit the chair under there. "One of the modifications I made to the house. Well, not me personally. There's a design company that fits out houses to make them wheelchair accessible." He gestured toward the cabinets. "Everything is within reach. Plus, I have a grabber for stuff that I don't use all that often."

"Did they widen the doorways too?"

"Oh, you noticed that? It's good to see being an accountant hasn't robbed you of *all* your faculties. And speaking of which…" Jamie grinned. "How does an accountant stay out of debt?"

"I have no idea, but I'm sure you're about to tell me."

"He learns to act his wage." Stephen groaned, but Jamie pressed ahead. "And did you hear about the woman who went to the doctor and was told she only had six months to live? 'Oh my God!' she said. 'What shall I do?' 'Marry an accountant,' suggested the doctor. 'Why?' asked the woman. 'Will that make me live longer?' 'No,' replied the doctor.' But it will *seem* longer.'"

Stephen groaned. "I think I'll go now. I'm not sure how much of this I can take without killing you."

Jamie laughed. "Okay. I'll play nice. No more jokes until after we've eaten."

"I was hoping for the rest of my visit, but I'll take whatever I can get." He opened the bottle and poured out two glasses, then handed one to Jamie. "Here's to old friends."

"Hey, less of the old," Jamie flung back at him. "But I'll drink to friendship." They clinked glasses, and he took a sip of the wine. It was cold and delicious. Jamie let out a happy sigh. "Thank God you have good taste in something. It almost makes up for your choice of rental car."

"Fuck you," Stephen said again with a grin. "Is dinner ready? Because I'm starved."

Jamie pointed to the dining table. "Go sit and I'll dish up." When Stephen opened his mouth, Jamie fired him a look. "And before you ask if you can help, I'm fine, thank you. If I need help, I'll ask for it."

"Which is how we got lost that summer, if I recall. Because *one* of us wouldn't ask a passerby for directions."

Jamie snorted. "That's a part of being male, didn't you know that? Men don't ask for directions, they just go miles out of their way." And that was how they'd ended up lost in a forest, with their parents going out of their minds with worry.

"We had some adventures, didn't we?"

Stephen's voice was warm.

"We sure did. And I suspect before the night is out, we're going to be doing a helluva lot of reminiscing about those times." Jamie could talk about their childhood till the cows came home. That was better than getting onto the topic of the accident. Jamie wasn't stupid. He knew they'd have to talk about it sooner or later.

Right then he was hoping for later.

Stephen let out a contented sigh. "Okay, I admit it. You can cook."

"Oh, sure. Don't believe me when *I* tell you that. Just wait until you've had three portions of lasagna to be *really* certain." Jamie had only had the one portion. He knew his limits. "There's ice cream if you have any room left."

Stephen's eyes sparkled. "Tell me you've got mint choc chip, and I'll love you forever."

Jamie laughed. "Oh, *I* see how it is. And yes, I do." They'd both loved it as kids, and it was a taste he'd never tired of. It was great to know Stephen was still a fan too. He rolled over to the freezer and opened it.

"By the way, I wasn't kidding. You really are a good cook."

Jamie flashed him a smile. "Why, thank you. I only have a small repertoire, and I tend to cook in batches then freeze them because I'm basically lazy, but I get by."

Stephen gazed at him with obvious affection. "You, lazy? Yeah right. You always worked your ass off at whatever you did, and I doubt that's changed." He gestured to the chair. "I've only got to watch you get around to know that." His eyes focused on it, and Jamie knew there was no getting away from the conversation.

Let's rip off the Band-aid and be done with it, okay?

It wasn't that he minded talking about the accident. He'd pushed all the pain and discomfort into a deep place long ago, locked the door, and thrown away the key. No, what he hated was the look in people's eyes when they listened. The look that spoke of pity.

Jamie didn't need anyone's pity. He didn't need people seeing him as less than whole, because he was doing *pretty damn fantastically*, thank you very much.

And he certainly didn't want to see that look in Stephen's eyes.

He took a mouthful of wine, inwardly praying that Stephen wouldn't prove to be like everyone else. Jamie had the awful feeling that might shatter him, and he didn't want to break in front of Stephen.

He's too important.

K.C. Wells

Chapter Six

Then he reconsidered. *If we're gonna do this, we'll do it my way.*

Jamie pulled the tub of ice cream from the freezer and closed the door. "I know you probably have a million questions, but if we're going to talk about this... you have tonight. That's it. That's all you get. So start thinking, because once you leave here, we don't discuss this again."

Stephen blinked. "Seriously?"

He nodded. "Do you need a pen and paper to write them all down?" He bit back a smile as he scooped ice cream into two bowls. "Chocolate sauce with yours?"

"Does a bear shit in the woods?"

Jamie cackled. "Oh my God. Your mom's face when you said that within earshot. I don't think I saw you for a week after that."

"I don't think I *sat down* for a week after that." Stephen walked over to collect his bowl, and Jamie laughed.

"Don't think I don't know what you're doing. You just wanna see how much sauce I'm pouring on."

"Duh." Stephen took the bottle and squeezed it, covering the vivid green ice cream with a rich dark brown. Instead of going back to the table, however, he laid his hand on Jamie's shoulder.

Jamie glanced up at him, and his throat seized.

Don't. Don't you fucking dare come out with some well-worn platitudes. Not you.

Stephen cleared his throat. "Do you think I could have another scoop of ice cream?"

For a moment Jamie wanted to laugh, until he realized Stephen had probably backpedaled after seeing his expression. That told him a lot about the man Stephen had become. He chuckled. "As it's you.... why not?" He dropped another ball of ice cream into the bowl, then shoved the tub back into the freezer.

They returned to the table, and Stephen didn't wait to dig in. Jamie ate slowly, his mind going over Stephen's likely questions. *Please don't ask about relationships.* That would be an extremely short conversation.

"The person who caused your accident... were they prosecuted?"

Jamie stilled. "Why—you gonna go teach him a lesson?"

"If I need to." Stephen's face darkened. "Don't get me started on people who drink and drive."

"Well, the law took care of him for you." Warmth spread through him, and he couldn't resist a comment. "Aww. You care enough to wanna beat the crap out of someone for me. I'm touched."

"Doof."

When Stephen's gaze flickered to his chair, Jamie gave him a frank stare. "Well? Where do you want to start?"

Stephen finished his spoonful of ice cream. "How bad was the accident? I mean, what did it do to you?"

Jamie held up his spoon, the bowl of it facing toward the floor. "Okay, this is my spine, and we'll say the bowl end is my ass. The back is made up of vertebrae." He smiled. "Can you remember that from Biology? I seem to recall you were too busy skimming the textbook trying to find pictures of the reproductive organs."

"Fuck you," Stephen said with a grin. "And yes, feather-brain, I know what vertebrae are."

"Okay then. The spine is made up of four sections, but the one we're talking about is the thoracic. That's the bit above where your ass begins. The vertebrae are numbered T1 to T12." He bit his lip. "T is for Thoracic, class."

Stephen merely gave him the finger.

"My injury occurred at T10, and it's what they call a complete injury. That means there's no sensation in my legs."

"So there really is no chance you'll walk again?"

Jamie shook his head.

Stephen studied at his upper body. "You seem pretty buff above the waist, if that's not too personal a comment."

It was the kind of remark to give a gay man hope, except Jamie was certain that was *not* the spirit in which it had been uttered. He smirked. "I'll take that as a compliment. And my instructor at the gym will be most gratified to hear that. He's worked me hard enough."

"You go to a gym?" Then Stephen stilled. "I'm sorry. I didn't mean to—"

"It's okay. I'm used to it by now." Jamie also

knew Stephen was still coming to terms with the situation. "Believe it or not, they let guys in wheelchairs into the gym too. And I exercise every day."

"I figured you did something. Watching you hefting that wheelchair into your car was pretty impressive."

"It's called practice. Now, any more questions?" Jamie knew there would be.

Stephen gestured toward the kitchen. "All these modifications... they can't have been cheap. This house could have been designed for you."

Jamie nodded. "Everything was paid for out of the compensation I got, plus grants that are available for people like me. They paid for the car too."

Stephen bit his lip. "If there's no feeling in your legs, what about... other parts?"

Jamie smirked. "Could you be a little more specific?" He had an inkling where this was leading. Sooner or later, people brought up the subject of his dick.

"Well... what about using the toilet? I mean, do you still know when you've got to... go?"

Jamie blinked. "Oh. Okay. This is where I'm lucky my injury was T10 and not below T12. That means—putting it bluntly—my ass stays shut unless I want it to open."

"Unless you *want* it to?"

"I have a routine. Every morning, I empty my bowels." When Stephen stared him, Jamie grinned. "Hey, *you* brought it up. Just don't expect me to share how I do that, because that would be gross."

"And what about peeing?"

Jamie arched his eyebrows. "My, you *do* want details, don't you? Well, my bladder still works. But that feeling you get that tells you that you need to pee? I don't get that. The signal doesn't get through. So every three to four hours, I get to catheterize myself."

"Ouch." Stephen winced.

Jamie waved his hand. "I'm used to it by now. And if I'm going someplace new, I have this handy little bag that I tape to my thigh." He chuckled. "Bet you're sorry you asked now, aren't you?"

Stephen laughed. "Well, it definitely comes under the heading of too much information." He looked down at his ice cream, then met Jamie's gaze. "But not enough to put me off my dessert." He resumed eating.

Jamie waited, but it soon became clear no more questions would be forthcoming. *He didn't ask.* Jamie was stunned for a moment. He'd felt certain the topic of relationships would have come up. He knew *he* wanted to know about Stephen's love life. *And he didn't ask about sex.* That was a new one. It was usually the first thing guys wanted to know. 'Can you still have sex? Can you still get a boner?'

But the absence of such queries gave him pause. *If he can ask questions about pee and shit, but not about my personal life...* There had to be a reason for it, and the most obvious one was that Stephen didn't want to invite similar questions.

Don't push it. Steer clear. Such questions would have to wait for another day.

He had another theory, however. *Stephen doesn't ask questions about my love life because he assumes I don't have one.* He wouldn't be the first to think that way. *Why is it most people have this misconception that people with disabilities can't have sex, don't want sex, or aren't interested in sex?*

Jamie was *definitely* interested in sex, but he was tired of being a solo act. He wanted a partner. During rehab, he'd asked one of the doctors what his disability would still allow him to do sexually. He'd received the disconcerting response to 'be realistic.'

Thank God for Jack. Jamie had met him at the gym a few years back, and they'd become good friends. Jack's wife was a paraplegic too, and Jamie being Jamie, he'd asked about sex. Thankfully, Jack hadn't minded discussing it, and the resulting conversation gave Jamie hope. There *were* people out there who would see the man and not only the wheelchair.

He just had to find one.

Jamie cleared his throat. "So are you looking for a place of your own?"

Stephen nodded. "Although nothing has jumped out at me so far. Plus, my budget is a little on the small side. That'll get better once I start working."

"Where are you looking?"

"All over Boston." Stephen smiled. "And the sooner the better. I'd gotten used to living away from home when I was studying."

Jamie couldn't hold back his cackle. "Aww, you mean you're not loving it, being back with your parents? Gee, I wonder why. Well, we'd better find you an alternative, and fast, before they drive you out of your mind." When the idea came to him, his first thought was to dismiss it. *He wouldn't want to*. Then Jamie reconsidered. *Fuck it. He can always say no, right?*

"If you really want to get out of their hair sooner rather than later, I do have a suggestion."

Stephen placed his spoon in his empty bowl. "Let's hear it. I'm open to ideas."

"How about you move in here? I won't charge you rent, but you can share the bills. We could split the groceries." He grinned again. "Of course, you'd have to share the chores too."

Stephen regarded him thoughtfully. "Move in here?"

"Why not? Just think of the benefits. We know each other. You can keep looking for a place but without your parents forever peeking over your shoulder. You'd have privacy." He gestured to the room. "Take a look at this place. I'm obviously not a slob. I've got a guest room I never use. We'd share the bathroom but that's okay, right?" It wasn't until that point that Jamie realized how much he wanted this. He loved his independence, but having someone else around the place?

That would be awesome.

Can a person be lonely without even realizing it?

But this wasn't just anyone. This was Stephen. And suddenly he *really* wanted Stephen to say yes.

Stephen smiled. "You're clearly house-trained. You can cook."

Jamie gave him a mock glare. "I won't be the only one cooking, I hope." He narrowed his gaze. "*Can* you cook?"

"Sure... as long as it's Ramen." Then Stephen burst into laughter. "Yeah, I can cook."

"This is sounding like a yes." Jamie mentally crossed all his fingers and toes.

Stephen nodded. "It's a yes, but with a proviso. You'd have to come visit my parents first. Before I tell them the good news. It's not like they aren't dying to see you anyway."

Jamie bit back a smile. "Do I have to pass a test or something before they'll let you move in with me?"

"Doof. I thought it would be good to... reconnect."

Jamie liked that. "I take it they know?" He didn't have to elaborate.

"Yeah."

Stephen's quietly uttered response told him plenty, but Jamie could deal with the sympathetic looks he felt certain would greet him.

"Can I see my room?"

Jamie laughed. "You don't waste time, do you? Sure. I'll give you the grand tour." He pushed himself away from the table and across the floor to the door. Stephen followed him. Jamie pointed to a closet door. "That's where I keep all my cleaning products and things like light bulbs. The top shelves are empty if you want to use them." Then he went on to the next door. "This is my room. Wanna take a peek?"

"Sure."

Jamie pushed open the door and entered, Stephen behind him. "See? I can even make my own bed."

"Well, that's one thing that's improved with age."

Jamie spun himself around and gave Stephen an indignant stare. "And what does that mean?"

"You couldn't make a bed to save your life. Your mom used to find all kinds of things stuffed under your comforter. Dirty socks, dirty briefs, your gym shorts, crackers…"

"Once. She found crackers *once*," Jamie declared. "And I did *not* use my bed as a laundry hamper, okay?"

Stephen opened the closet and let out a loud gasp. "Oh my God. Jamie got organized."

"Bastard." Jamie headed out of the room. "Come see the bathroom. I need to show you the shower."

Stephen followed him into the small room. Jamie pointed to the commode. "That's the same height as my chair, only the handle slips down so I can transfer myself onto it. So don't go adjusting anything when you move it, okay?"

"Got it."

Jamie pulled back the shower curtain. "I don't know if you like taking baths or showers. I only shower, and I sit on that." He pointed to the chair. "If you take a bath, put everything back where you found it. And that includes the massager if you take a shower. It hangs down for a reason."

"Got it." Stephen gazed at the room.

Jamie didn't need to be a mind reader to know what was going on inside Stephen's head. "It's okay," he said quietly. "I know it will take some getting used to, but this is my life now, and I'm fine with that. If you feel you can't live with all this, then tell me now." It was better to know before they went any further.

Stephen shook his head. "I'm not going to change my mind. It's just…" He sighed. "I think you're amazing."

Jamie blinked. "Why?"

"Because you've taken all this in your stride. Because you're still Jamie, despite everything that's happened."

Jamie smiled. "Believe me, I wasn't always like this. But I wasn't going to let it defeat me, and that meant finding a way forward." He straightened in his chair. "Now… wanna see your room? It's next door."

As he wheeled into the guest room, Jamie relaxed a little.

Looks like I've gotten myself a roommate.

There would be problems initially, he was sure of that, but nothing they couldn't adapt to. And they would both need to adapt. It wasn't until Stephen was testing the bed for firmness that a thought occurred to him.

What if he wants to bring a girl home?

Not that Jamie would tell Stephen he couldn't. He would have to invest in earplugs and work really hard at not being jealous as hell.

Besides, think positively. I could have a guy in my room, right? We could be having hot, passionate sex all night long.

Yeah right. He was almost deafened by the sound of the pigs' wings as they flew past the house.

It wasn't until later that he knew what would *really* kill him if Stephen brought a girl home, and when it hit him, it made his chest tighten.

Jamie wanted to be the one in Stephen's bed.

Chapter Seven

Stephen sniffed the air as he stepped into the kitchen. "That smells so good."

Mom laughed. "Anything that's *food* smells good to you. Although I recall you gagging one time when I bought that really strong cheese."

He groaned. "It smelled like sweaty feet. And you wanted me to *eat* it." He gazed at the countertops. "Wow. You really pulled out all the stops for this lunch." Not only had she made her delicious meatloaf, there was mac and cheese, her melt-in-the-mouth garlic roasted potatoes, broccoli, her parmesan-garlic carrots, peas, and mashed potatoes. Not to mention her gravy. He chuckled. "Jamie had better be wearing something with an elasticated waistband."

She frowned. "Is it too much?"

Stephen patted her arm. "You know none of it will go to waste. Dad loves meatloaf sandwiches, for one thing. And since when did you *ever* throw away any of your mac and cheese?"

Mom's frown faded, and she smiled. "I wanted it to be special, after all this time."

Stephen remembered how much Jamie had loved his mom's cooking. "He's not changed that much. He'll love whatever you put in front of him."

She laughed. "I always said he had a tapeworm. He ate so much and yet he was as skinny as a rake."

"There's a Corvette pulling onto the driveway," Dad called out from the living room.

"That'll be Jamie," Stephen told him, heading for the front door.

"But he's not driving it, is he?"

Stephen ignored the question and opened the door, just as Jamie switched off the engine. He walked out to the car, parked behind his Toyota. "I hope you're hungry. Mom seems to be expecting the five thousand for lunch."

"As long as it's gonna be more than loaves and fishes, I'm good." Jamie reached into the back of the car and began assembling the wheelchair next to him. Stephen was about to offer help when he reconsidered. Jamie was more than capable. He waited as Jamie transferred himself to the chair.

"Oh, dear Lord, I can smell it from here." Jamie's face erupted into a rapturous smile. "Tell me she's made some of my favorites?"

Stephen snorted. "She's certainly killed the fatted calf."

Jamie arched his eyebrows. "You're throwing around a lot of Biblical references. Did you find God in California?"

"Nah. He was always too busy surfing."

Jamie cackled. "I like that image. God on a board." He pointed to the passenger seat. "There's a bunch of flowers for your mom. Can you grab 'em?"

"Sure." Stephen picked up the bouquet, inhaling their sublime fragrance. "She'll love these."

"That's the general idea." Jamie locked the car and wheeled toward the house. Then he came to a dead stop with a smirk. "Houston, we have a problem."

Stephen frowned as he followed Jamie's gaze.

"Aw crap."

Jamie patted his arm. "It's fine. I didn't expect you to build me a ramp, okay? But I *will* need a bit of help lifting the chair up those steps."

"Sure." Stephen went to the door. "Dad? Can you come here a minute?" Seconds later his dad was there, his eyes wide when he saw Jamie. Stephen pointed to the chair. "If I take the back, can you take the front? Between us we can manage it."

"Of course." Dad hurried outside as Jamie turned himself around, his back to the door.

He smirked. "Want me to hold the flowers? Because I have visions of you crushing them while you're trying to maneuver me."

"Here." Stephen handed them over, and Jamie held onto them. Stephen guided the chair to the steps.

"You ever done this before?" Jamie asked him.

"Er, no."

"Okay then. Who's stronger, you or your dad?"

"Him," Dad said without hesitation.

"Then you're in the right places." Jamie gave instructions, and between them, they lifted and rolled the wheelchair up onto the first step. When they reached the top, Stephen gently lowered the chair until all four wheels were down.

Jamie peered at the ground. "Oh my God. I'm gonna get altitude sickness, we're so high up."

Stephen hit him on the arm. "Behave." His dad raised his eyebrows at that.

Jamie laughed. "It's okay, Mr. Taylor. I'm used to the abuse. You should see what he did to me when we were kids. Torture, I'm telling you!"

His dad opened and closed his mouth, plainly at

a loss for words. Stephen stood to one side while Jamie swung himself around, then pointed to the living room. "Come in here. Lunch is nearly ready."

Jamie paused at the doorway, as if mentally assessing the gap, then carefully wheeled himself into the room. "Any narrower, and I'd have to put the chair on a diet," he joked. Dad and Stephen followed him, and once inside, Dad stood by the fireplace, giving Jamie glances before looking away and clearing his throat.

Mom came into the room and stopped dead at the sight of Jamie. "Oh. Jamie. You're here."

Jamie smiled. "Yup. Hi there, Mrs. T. You haven't changed a bit."

Mom gave a half smile. "Thanks. You look… older."

Jamie held out the flowers. "Thanks for the invite."

"Oh. How lovely." Mom took them, immediately setting them down on the side table. "Well. This is nice."

Stephen had had enough of the awkward atmosphere, but before he could say a word, Jamie grinned. "Aw, don't I rate a hug anymore?"

His words seemed to provide a catalyst, and Mom lurched forward, bending over to put her arms around Jamie's shoulders. "Hi, Jamie. It's good to see you again." Her voice held her usual warmth, and Stephen gave an internal sigh of relief. Dad stepped forward, his hand outstretched, and Jamie shook it vigorously.

"Good to see you too, sir. I see you've still got that firm grip. I've met some folks where shaking their hand is like handling a limp lettuce."

Mom chuckled. "You haven't changed either. I hope you're hungry."

Jamie's eyes lit up. "Does a bear sh—" He coughed. "Yes, ma'am, I'm starving." Mom bit her lip.

"No change there either," Dad commented with a smile.

Stephen couldn't resist. "Hey, Mom. You're not gonna believe this, but Jamie can cook."

She arched her eyebrows. "Well, anything would be a step up from his mud pies."

"Hey, I made *great* mud pies," Jamie exclaimed. "There was the perfect amount of mud in each one."

"Yes, but you weren't supposed to *eat* them," Mom retorted.

"I was six!" Jamie looked at Stephen. "Your mom's got a memory like mine. This could be an embarrassing lunch."

"I'm sure she'll go easy on you. Won't you, Mom?" Stephen grinned. He wanted the years to melt away as they had done when he'd eaten at Jamie's place.

"Hey, I can put up with *anything* if I get to taste your mom's cooking again," Jamie said, his eyes sparkling.

Mom laughed. "Then you're going to be very happy. I have three words for you—mac and cheese."

Jamie groaned. "Mrs. T, I love you."

Mom was still laughing as she led Jamie into the dining room.

Jamie pushed away his plate. "I don't think I'm gonna eat for a week. That was awesome."

Dad peered into one of the bowls in the center of the table. "There's still some mashed potatoes left. And some of the garlic roasts too."

Stephen had to laugh at the indecision in Jamie's expression. "But if you eat those, you definitely won't have room for dessert."

Jamie stilled. "There's dessert?"

Mom nodded. "Peach cobbler. With ice cream."

Jamie threw his hands up in the air. "No fair. As if any sane man could resist your peach cobbler."

"I take it that means you'd like some?"

"Just a little?" Jamie held his fingers about an inch apart, but then widened them to three or four.

Mom burst into a peal of laughter. "That's the Jamie I remember." She got up from the table and went into the kitchen.

"So Jamie, I have to ask," Dad said as he helped himself to one more garlic roasted potato. "Why a Corvette?"

Jamie frowned. "Why not?"

"Yes, but surely… I mean, there must be other cars out there that are more… practical for you."

Jamie's eyes sparkled. "But where's the fun in being practical? And I love driving her. That baby can *move*." He gave the last potato a look of sheer longing. "You gonna eat that?"

Dad laughed. "Have at it."

"How is Marie?" Jamie asked Dad after swallowing his mouthful of potato with a noise that spoke of utter bliss.

Dad's face glowed. "She's doing great. She's married, with a couple of kids. They live in Carmel-by-the-sea. It's a fine place to bring up kids."

Jamie let out a happy sigh. "I'm glad. Tell her I said hi when you next speak to her. How old are the kids?"

"Natasha is six and Declan is three."

Stephen said nothing. Marie hadn't shared her news yet.

Jamie smiled. "That's wonderful. I'd like to have kids one day."

Dad frowned. "But surely… I mean, that would be difficult, right?" He cleared his throat. As he got up from the table, a pile of dishes in his hand, Jamie caught Stephen's gaze and unseen by his dad he rolled his eyes.

Stephen gazed at him in surprise. He waited until Dad had left the room. "You mean that? You really want kids?"

Jamie blinked. "Of course. Why not? I think I'd make a great dad. Imagine what fun my kids would have, sitting on their dad's knee while he went for a roll." He grinned, but then his expression became more serious. "People in a much worse state than me have fathered kids, and they manage fine. Why, I saw this TV show about a woman in the UK with no arms, and *she's* got kids. And she's a great mom. It all depends on how you look at things."

"I guess." Stephen had always been in awe of Jamie's positivity when they were children. It was as if there was something inside him that made him constantly see the bright side. His grandma used to call it 'Jamie's Pollyanna Gene.'

Stephen did *not* possess such a gene.

Mom came back into the room with the dish of cobbler, and all conversation ceased, except for Jamie's moans of delight, which had Stephen chuckling.

Mom went to make the coffee, and Dad leaned back in his chair. "Stephen says you have a house. I think that's admirable."

Jamie frowned. "Why? *You* have a house. That's what people do, right? Set up home?"

"Yes, but… it can't be easy."

Jamie shrugged. "I don't see why having a house would be difficult. Of course, my life is about to change, and that promises to be interesting. Doesn't it, Stephen?" Jamie gave him a knowing glance.

"Oh? Why's that?" Dad asked. "Stephen?"

Shit. Stephen was going to wait until after the coffee, but seeing as Jamie had gotten the ball rolling… He wasn't really sure why he hadn't brought it up already. Mom walked in with the tray containing the coffee pot and cups and saucers.

No time like the present.

"Mom? Dad? I know I said I was going to look for a house, but I've come to a decision." Stephen straightened in his chair. "I'm going to wait a while longer, until I can afford something I really want, instead of making do with what fits my budget right now."

"Does that mean you're going to finally unpack?" Mom asked. "You can't keep living out of boxes and suitcases, not if you're going to stay here."

"Well, actually… I'm going to move in with Jamie. He's asked me to be his roommate. So I won't be under your feet any longer," Stephen told her.

Her brow furrowed. "You're not under my feet now. But—"

"Is this a good idea?" Dad interjected. "It sounds to me like Jamie has his own… routines. Surely having you living there might make things… awkward for him."

"You *can* talk to me about this, you know." Jamie's expression was neutral. "I mean, I'm sitting right here. And I wouldn't have made the offer if I thought Stephen would be a pain to live with." His lips twitched. "Of course, if he starts leaving wet towels on the bathroom floor, not putting the cap back on the toothpaste, and using up all the hot water, then we might have to reassess the situation." He smiled. "I'll give him a trial period, how's that?"

Stephen had to laugh. "Okay, Mr. Neatness. I promise not to be a slob, all right?"

"Have you really thought about this, Jamie?" Mom asked. "You're used to living alone, after all."

"Which is why it'll be awesome to have Stephen living there." Jamie gave him a warm glance. "It's not like we're strangers, right? And it'll be good to have someone there to help me clean up after the wild parties I throw once a week. We'll just have to keep an eye on the noise level. The neighbors called the cops last time."

Mom and Dad stared at Jamie in obvious bewilderment, but Stephen cackled. "He's yanking your chain. Aren't you?"

Jamie gave a sheepish grin. "Yeah. I don't have that exciting a life, I promise. But it *will* be wonderful to have Stephen there."

Faced with Jamie's obvious enthusiasm for the plan, Stephen knew his mom wouldn't have the heart to put any more obstacles in their path. She sighed. "You two. I swear—"

Jamie let out a gasp of mock horror. "Surely not. Unless living in California got you into bad ways?"

She speared him with a look. "Jamie Lithgow, you haven't changed one bit."

He preened. "I know. Great, isn't it?" He peered at the coffee pot. "*Now* can I have some coffee?"

Mom laughed as she poured coffee into the cups. "Your poor neighbors. They won't know what hit them."

"Hey!" Stephen gave her an indignant stare.

Mom rolled her eyes. "I can see it now. You two were always getting into trouble when you were kids."

"But I'm twenty-six," Stephen protested. "I'm mature."

Jamie chuckled. "Yeah, right." His parents laughed at that.

Stephen helped himself to coffee, thankful that they'd crossed that hurdle. All he had to do now was move all his stuff into Jamie's house, and then get used to being a roommate.

He couldn't wait.

Chapter Eight

"Is that the last one?" Jamie called from the door.

Stephen closed the trunk. "That's it. Everything I own is currently sitting in boxes in your living room." He locked the car and headed for the house.

"Hey, it's *your* living room too now," Jamie said with a smile. "And unloading the car was the easy part. I could help with that, a little. Now you get to unpack." His eyes twinkled. "Been there, done that, not doing it again, even for you."

Stephen followed him into the house, closing the door behind him. "I guess I'd better check to see where it's all going." Although it might have been a good idea to do that first. He'd been buzzing all week about the prospect of moving in, so much so that his dad had made some comment about keeping his mind on the job. Which was fair enough—Stephen *was* interviewing prospective employees, after all. It was like being a little kid again, and the holidays were drawing closer. Stephen hadn't realized until that Sunday lunch, just how much he wanted to be out of his parents' hair—and their sight.

Talk about cramping my style. Not that Stephen was about to go hooking up with anyone—he still had the mental scars from that last time—but at least he had the option, should the opportunity present itself.

He walked into his room and straight into the closet. It wasn't huge by any means, and he had the sinking feeling he wasn't going to fit all his clothes in there. One look at the bedroom confirmed his fears.

"This isn't going to work," he muttered.

"What isn't?" Jamie came into the room.

"There's no way I can get all my stuff in here. There's not enough storage." Why hadn't he thought about that?

"Then we go shopping and buy *more* storage," Jamie replied practically. "No problem."

"Yeah, but that all takes time and effort."

Jamie chuckled. "So what? We do it once, it's done. Like I said, no biggie." He surveyed the space. "Now, what say we start bringing boxes in here?"

"I should've brought them straight in here," Stephen groused. "Now I've got to do the job twice."

Jamie snorted. "You were in a hurry to get in here. I'll go make sure there's plenty of coffee, while you make a start. Then you can use me as a willing packhorse if you like. I can only carry one box at a time, however." He wheeled himself out of the room.

Stephen shook his head. It was like when they were kids. Wherever Stephen had seen a problem, Jamie had come up with a solution.

Maybe I should look at this situation and think, 'Now what would Jamie do?' The thought made him smile. He gazed at the furniture, what little there was of it, and tried to visualize how it would look rearranged.

"Hey, Jamie! Can I move stuff around in here?"

He caught Jamie's laughter. "It's your room, dude. Do what you like with it. Just don't go moving anything else in the house. I kinda like things how they are, okay?"

That made things easier. The desk Jamie had in there would be great under the window, rather than stuck in the corner. It made sense to move furniture before he started bringing in boxes. Stephen tried to lift it, but the wooden desk was way too heavy, so he resorted to dragging it across the floor.

He looked down and came to an abrupt halt. *Aw fuck.*

"Coffee's on." Jamie came into the bedroom, then stopped. "What's wrong?"

Stephen sighed. "I ruined your floor." He looked at the scratches on the hardwood, where one of the desk legs had left its mark.

Jamie followed his gaze and chuckled. "It's not the end of the world, okay? It's a scratch. It's a fact of life. Floors get scratched unless you cover 'em with rugs."

"But I haven't even been in the place five minutes and already I'm spoiling it."

Jamie rolled over to him and caught Stephen's hand. "Hey," he said, his voice soft. "It's just stuff, okay? And if you really want to move this, I'll get Rob next door to come over. He's the one who usually helps out if I can't do something." His eyes twinkled. "Not that it happens very often. And to be honest, I only invite him in because he makes the place look pretty. I'll give him a call."

Before Stephen could protest, Jamie had left the room. It was only then that his words sank in. *Rob makes the place look pretty?* It seemed an odd thing to say. Then again, Jamie was prone to coming out with odd sayings. Stephen hadn't forgotten being referred to as a tall drink of water. Definitely not what he'd expected. *Does he know how gay it makes him sound?* Then he smiled to himself. He got the impression Jamie wouldn't give a shit how something made him sound. He said whatever was on his mind, and people had to deal with it.

Stephen wished he could be more like that.

Jamie rejoined him, and Stephen sat on the bed, a mug of coffee on the nightstand, while he and Jamie looked online for a chest of drawers. Jamie quickly found the perfect one, and Stephen ordered it. He stared at the scratched floor. "I'm sorry about that."

Jamie let out a growling sound. "Do I have to beat you? It's just a scratch. And it's *my* floor, for Christ's sake. If *I'm* not getting all stressed out about it, neither should you. So either cover it with a rug, furniture, or shut the fuck up about it." He grinned. "You got that?"

"Yeah," Stephen said with some reluctance. Jamie gave him a mock glare and he chuckled. "Okay, okay, I've got it."

"That's better. And by the way? There are kits for repairing scratches in wooden floors, and I just ordered one." Jamie looked smug. "So we're not gonna mention that again today, you hear? Now, Rob said he'll be over in an hour, so what can we get done before then?"

"We?"

Jamie rolled his eyes. "Well, duh. Clearly you need someone to keep an eye on you. And I can put clothes on hangers or on shelves. Low shelves, naturally." He grinned again. "Come on, dude. Those boxes won't move themselves, right? And I promise not to make fun of your taste in clothes."

Stephen snorted. "I've heard *that* before."

Jamie widened his eyes. "Hey, since when have I ever broken a promise?"

He stroked his chin. "Gee, let's see. 'I promise I won't tell your mom it was *you* who ate all the strawberries.'"

"One time, you bastard."

"No, that's only the first one that comes to mind. There *were* other times." Then Stephen relented. "But I guess you letting me move in sort of wipes the slate clean."

"Oh, thanks." Jamie's voice was heavy with sarcasm. Then he gave Stephen a sideways glance. "Clean slate, huh? I'd better come up with some new shit then."

Stephen speared him with a look. "How about you *don't*, hmm? Maybe act like a grown-up?"

Jamie let out a loud snort. "But where's the fun in that? Now, if you'll excuse me, I'll go find a box that A, I can reach, and B, I can carry. Otherwise, we'll still be doing this come nightfall. Time's a-wastin', like your grandma used to say." And with that, he wheeled himself out of the room.

Stephen smiled to himself. One thing about living with Jamie—it sure as shit wasn't going to be dull.

"I thought you ate healthily," Stephen commented as he shut the door, a pizza box in his hand. "Since when is pizza healthy?"

Jamie stared at him. "Did *you* wanna cook tonight, after dealing with all those boxes, bags and suitcases? No? Well, newsflash—neither did I. We've earned this. And there are some bottles of beer in the refrigerator with our names on them. I think we've earned them too."

"We should've asked Rob if he wanted to stay for dinner," Stephen said as he inhaled the wonderful aroma spilling forth from the pizza box. Rob had turned out to be a big guy with a whole lotta muscles, who'd moved the desk like it was made of cardboard. Stephen could understand why Jamie had noticed Rob's looks—Rob was *very* easy on the eye.

Jamie laughed. "No way. I've seen how he eats. I went to his place once for a barbecue. I think he ate half a pig. He must burn it all off at the gym, which is where he spends a lot of his time."

"And how do you know that?"

Jamie grinned. "There's this great bakery next door to his gym. They do the most amazing cinnamon rolls. Rob always brings me one when he goes there." He patted his belly. "Then I get to work it off, but trust me, it's worth it."

Stephen followed Jamie into the kitchen, where he retrieved the beers while Stephen grabbed paper napkins for the pizza. Then they went over to the table. When he opened the box, Stephen groaned. "There are mushrooms on it. I should've said, no mushrooms." He'd let Jamie go ahead and order, not even considering the toppings.

Jamie chuckled. "So there are mushrooms on it. Big fucking deal." He rolled his eyes. "The world's not gonna end because of a few mushrooms. I'll pick them all off and stick them on my side of the pizza." His eyes glittered. "At least this way I guarantee myself half." He helped himself to a slice, smacking his lips.

Stephen stared at him. "How do you do that?"

"Do what?" Jamie said, his mouth full. He swallowed. "Sorry about that."

"How do you *always* see the freaking bright side? Even when we were kids, you were the same. Yet I'd have thought—" He clammed up, unwilling to continue for fear of putting his foot in it.

Jamie regarded him thoughtfully. "Finish your sentence. *What* would you have thought?"

There was no backing out now.

"I don't get it. If what happened to you had happened to *me*, I wouldn't cope with it the way you have. I watch you get around in that chair, laughing, joking, finding fun in life…"

Jamie cocked his head to one side. "So you think I'm coping well?"

"Well, aren't you?" Stephen stared at him. "*Look* at you. You could be the poster boy for Happy." It was rare to find him without a smile or a chuckle.

Jamie put down his pizza slice and wiped his fingers on a napkin, before looking Stephen in the eye. "You keep forgetting something. You're seeing me now, eight years after the accident. You didn't see me in the months right after it happened. The *year* after, if it comes to that."

"So tell me how you were then." Because Stephen wanted to know. Marie's words were burned into his memory. *What if Jamie really is putting on a brave face for the world, for me?*

Jamie said nothing for a moment, but scrutinized Stephen's face, as if he was internally debating what to say. Then he let out a heavy sigh.

"What do you want to know? How when I lay in that hospital bed, I thought my life was over at eighteen years old? How I thought I could never be happy again? Do you want to hear how I grieved?" Jamie's voice quavered. "How I refused to accept what the doctors were telling me? How I lashed out at my nurses, my parents? Because I went through *all* of those things, and more."

"I've never seen you angry," Stephen said, his heart aching for his friend.

"Trust me, it wasn't pretty. And my heart breaks now when I recall my mom's face. She didn't deserve that. Neither of them did. They helped me so much. At the beginning I didn't believe the doctors when they said the paralysis was permanent. I didn't want to eat. I felt dejected. Depressed. Angry."

"Did you blame yourself for the accident?"

Jamie shook his head. "There was nothing I could've done, but you'd better believe I cursed the drunken bastard who put me in that hospital bed." His face tightened. "You know I asked if you found God out in California? Well, for weeks after the diagnosis, I was trying to do deals with Him. 'Make me walk again and I'll do this, I'll do that.' You get the picture. Only, He wasn't listening. Either that, or He wasn't there to hear me in the first place. And as the weeks and months went by, I acted like I'd accepted the situation, but you know what? It was a fucking lie. The words may have left my mouth, but what was in my head was that my hard work in therapy was going to lead to recovery. I tried to fool myself." Jamie swallowed, then drew in a deep

breath. "You have no idea how much work, how much conscious *effort* it takes to maintain a positive outlook. Because it would be all too easy to let my subconscious take control." He straightened in his chair. "I've moved on, okay? I don't deny or reject those feelings I had, because at the time they were valid. But I came to a decision long ago. I realized my future wouldn't be healthy if I continued thinking like that, so—"

"So you pushed those thoughts away," Stephen concluded. "Because it's not in your nature to stay down for long." He smiled. "Eat your pizza before it gets cold."

Jamie laughed. "Nothing wrong with cold pizza." But he shivered.

Stephen took Jamie's hand in his. "Thank you for letting me in. And I'm not talking about this house."

Jamie lowered his gaze to look at their hands. "I knew I'd tell you sooner or later. I just hadn't figured on how soon."

Stephen squeezed his hand. "The other day I said you were amazing. For the record? I think you leave amazing in your dust."

Jamie's face flushed as he raised his chin to look Stephen in the eye. "Seeing as we're being honest?" He smiled. "I'm glad I let you in too. Now let's eat."

They ate until not even a crumb remained, and Stephen had a nice buzz going on from his second bottle of beer. Jamie declined another, saying he didn't drink all that much.

"I think I'll watch a movie in my room. Wanna join me?"

Stephen smiled. "What are you thinking of watching?"

"Oh, something with car chases that gets the ol' blood pumping." Jamie speared him with a look. "No food, okay? I do *not* want to be finding cookie crumbs or chips stuck in my ass in the morning."

Stephen laughed. "Okay. Just be prepared. I'm wiped out. I might not make it to the end of the movie."

Jamie's grin was as wide as ever. "That's fine. You snore, and you'll probably wake up on the floor." He pointed to the pizza box and bottles. "You deal with the trash, and I'll go set up the TV." He rolled away from the table.

Stephen collected the trash and took it to the recycling box Jamie kept by the back door. It had been a long day, but he'd accomplished a lot. He had a new home, and Jamie was going to be a great roommate. After hearing him talk about all the pain he'd gone through, Stephen had come to realize how strong Jamie truly was.

And how thankful Stephen was for choosing to go to the pond that day.

Why couldn't one *of the guys I met have been like you?* Because Stephen's life could have been so different. *If I'd met someone like Jamie out there, I'd have fallen for him in a heartbeat.*

Except that was the problem. He'd fallen for *several* guys that fast. And the story was always the same. Great sex to start off with, euphoria that he'd found someone to connect with, and then little by little, their true natures emerged, submerging his hopes and dreams in a deep, stinking mess of one abusive relationship after another.

You think I'd have learned my lesson, right? But I kept on repeating the same stupid mistake.

Well, no more. That life was over. He'd left it behind in California.

And then it struck him with all the force of a battering ram.

New life, sure, but one thing hasn't changed— me. What if the problem was me all along? What if I'm the kind of guy who puts out some sort of signal that only attracts bastards?

If that was the case, then maybe it was time to consider staying single. Unless he met a Jamie-clone, of course.

Yeah right.

K.C. Wells

Chapter Nine

"Jamie. *Jamie*."

He turned his head toward the living room door. "Hmm?" He'd gotten lost in the code for the new website he'd started working on the previous week.

Stephen chuckled. "Earth to Jamie, come in Jamie. I've been asking you for the last couple of minutes if there's anything we need. I can always shop on my way home from work."

Jamie shook his head. "We're good. Unless…." He flashed Stephen a grin.

Stephen rolled his eyes. "What is it? More ice cream? Cinnamon rolls? Isn't your buddy Rob going to feed that particular habit at some point today?"

"I was *gonna* say, we need more toilet cleaner." He paused. "*Then* I was gonna say buy more ice cream."

"Sure. Mint choc or Rocky Road?"

Jamie rolled his eyes. "Both. Duh."

Stephen narrowed his gaze. "Have you had breakfast?"

"No—*Mom.*" He'd switched on his PC to take a look at something, and that had been it, down the rabbit hole he went. "I'll go eat now, okay? Now go be a good little accountant and have an exciting day." He cackled. "Except that'd be wrong on both counts, 'cause you ain't little in anyone's book, and we all know accounting is as dull as—"

"Can it. I'm out of here before you pull yet another accounting joke from your vast repertoire."

Jamie gave him a wide-eyed stare. "But I'm only up to #56. I've got *lots* more to share."

Stephen merely laughed and gave him a wave. "See you this evening." And then he was gone.

Jamie smiled to himself. Stephen had moved in on Saturday, and it already felt like he was part of the furniture. It was a good start, except for one thing. Jamie still hadn't managed to catch him coming out of the shower. Because what was the point of living with a gorgeous man if he didn't get the chance to see him in the nude? Not that it was a serious wish.

Okay, maybe it was. Jamie was honest enough to admit that much.

His phone buzzed as he was wheeling himself into the kitchen. He peered at the screen and clicked on Answer. "Hey. Good morning."

"You haven't killed each other yet, then?" He could hear the laughter in Mom's voice.

"Give it time. We're only on day three. He's just left for the office."

"You think it'll work out?"

Jamie thought it would work out fine. "Yeah. Now, what can I do for you?" Mom was *not* one to call with no reason.

"I'm calling because *someone* hasn't told me he's coming to the party on Saturday."

"Aw, crap. *This* Saturday?"

"Yes, dear. This Saturday. Which coincidentally happens to be the same day as our silver wedding anniversary. Imagine that."

He sighed. "I'm sorry. It slipped my mind, what

with Stephen suddenly strolling back into my life."

"And speaking of Stephen… you *are* bringing him along, aren't you? Seeing as we have yet to lay eyes on him."

"That's cruel. Why would I want to subject him to all my family, most of whom I haven't seen since I was little? And don't tell me I'm wrong, because Liz showed me the guest list months ago." Jamie knew why he'd conveniently put off confirming his appearance at the party. Why on earth would he want to meet lots of relatives who were bound to stare at his chair and lapse into awkward silences, make sympathetic noises, or even worse, comments?

Then he reconsidered. Having Stephen there would improve the situation. At least he'd have an ally: his parents would be too busy to run any interference.

"You don't *have* to come."

Jamie didn't miss the note of hurt. As if he'd disappoint her.

"I'll be there," he reassured her. "And when Stephen gets home tonight, I'll ask him, okay?"

"It would be great to see him."

Jamie chuckled. "You've missed your second son, haven't you?" When they were kids, Liz used to tease him that Mom and Dad loved Stephen more than they loved Jamie.

"Of course I have. I want to hear all about his life in California."

That made two of them. Stephen hadn't shared all that much about it. Jamie was beginning to get the feeling his friend was hiding something.

"Has he changed much? Apart from the whole growing tall thing."

Jamie wasn't sure if he could put his feelings into words. "You remember how much we used to laugh when we were together?"

Mom chuckled. "I recall me frequently telling you two to stop laughing and go to sleep, every time he stayed over."

"Well… he still makes me laugh, but…" Jamie thought back to their conversation the day Stephen moved in. "Would you say we were alike back then?"

Mom laughed. "No, not at all. Okay, so you liked lots of the same things, but you were two very different children."

"I think we still are, only now the difference is more… pronounced."

"That's bound to happen. You're adults. You've both been through different experiences." A pause. "One thing that hasn't changed about you, sweetheart? You're still my sunshine boy. My wonderful son who sees the positive in every situation."

And just like that, she'd nailed it.

"Stephen doesn't. It's like, his default is to see the worst. Okay, maybe I'm exaggerating, but the littlest things happen, and he makes mountains out of molehills." He hadn't been like that as a kid.

"Honey, he's your opposite, that's all. Maybe he's a 'glass-half-empty' kind of man. Not all of us can be like you."

He didn't want to tell her how hard he worked to be so positive. It was a mindset, and occasionally he faltered, but he always got back into it.

"Maybe if he spends more time around you, your attitude will rub off on him," Mom suggested.

Jamie had to smile at that. "You think?"

Mom laughed. "I defy anyone to be around you for any length of time and not be affected by your—"

"Sunshine?" It had always been her word for his positive nature.

"Yes, sweetheart, your sunshine. Now, I'll let you get on with your day, and I can't wait to see you on Saturday. *With* Stephen."

Jamie got the message. "I'll make sure he's there." Not that he thought Stephen would object to seeing his parents. *He might balk at the idea of a house full of relatives though.* They said goodbye, and he disconnected. As he poured cereal into a bowl, Jamie got to wondering about Stephen.

What happened to make him like this? Jamie firmly believed most people's lives were shaped by their circumstances. *We all have a choice to accept those circumstances or rail against them.* He'd chosen to fight the depression, the anger, the tendency to lapse into self-pity.

Jamie had chosen to live life to the full. Was it wrong that he wanted Stephen to do the same?

Jamie lay on his stomach on the bed, pushing his upper body up with his arms. It was one of a series of stretches he did every day. Hip flexors had a tendency to tighten, and he worked on them to prevent that. When that set was done, he rolled onto his back and pulled one knee up to his chest and held it there.

"You busy?" Stephen called through the closed door.

"Kind of, but you can come in."

Stephen came into the room and stopped dead at the sight. "Oh. You *are* busy."

Jamie chuckled. "Sit on that chair and talk. I can talk and do stretches at the same time, you know." He released his leg and did the same with the other. He still had fourteen more to go.

After a moment he grew conscious of Stephen's gaze. Jamie wore a pair of shorts, his chest bare. *Like what you see, Stephen?* Then he gave himself a mental kick. *Lord, I have to stop these thoughts.* And that included his nocturnal fantasies too, even if they *were* PG-rated. He'd lie in bed, thinking about Stephen holding him, kissing him.

What Jamie wouldn't give to be on the receiving end of a really good, long, toe-curling kiss from Stephen.

Except I can't curl 'em anymore, remember? But the thought was there.

"How often do you do these?" Stephen asked as he sat.

"Every day." Jamie gave him a glance. "Well, what's up? Have you changed your mind already about going to the party?"

Stephen laughed. "Doof. Of course I haven't. It'll be awesome to see your folks again. I can't wait to see how Liz turned out."

"Liz is all loved up," Jamie said with a smile as he pulled himself into a sitting position. "Phil's a great

guy, and I'm really happy for her. The last guy she dated was an asshole." He brought his knee up to his chest, holding onto his ankle as he pushed the knee away for thirty seconds. Then he noticed
Stephen had gone quiet. Stephen was staring at Jamie, clearly lost in thought. "Okay, where did you go to?" Jamie teased.

"I was thinking… your legs look okay."

Jamie smiled. "Thank you. I work hard to make sure they do. These stretches work the inside and outside of the leg." He continued, aware once more of Stephen's intense scrutiny. Jamie didn't mind one bit. The hard part was resisting the urge to flex for him.

"Why was he an asshole?"

It took Jamie a second or two to join the dots. "Oh. Liz. Right. Yeah, well, he was abusive. We didn't find out until she finally walked away from him." Jamie scowled. "Wish I could get my hands on him." He shook his head. "Why do people stay with assholes like that? I mean, she's smart. Why did she stick it out as long as she did?"

"Maybe she thought no one else would be interested in her. That at least being in the relationship was better than being alone. Maybe she thought the abuse was her fault. He might have promised that he'd change, and she believed him. Maybe she thought things would get better." He paused. "There *are* people who think holding onto something makes them strong, when sometimes it takes more strength to let go."

Jamie stilled and gazed at Stephen. "That's quite profound." Not to mention endearing. There was a sweet, gentle man hiding behind that sometimes pessimistic exterior.

Stephen shrugged. "Must have read it somewhere. Anyway, I came in to ask if you wanted some hot chocolate before bed. I feel like making some."

"That would be great. It would be even better if you drank yours in here while I finish up." When Stephen gave him a quizzical glance, Jamie smiled. "I'm in the mood for company."

"Sure." Stephen got up and left the room.

Jamie sat up against the pillows and lifted one leg over the other to work on his toes and ankles, his mind going over Stephen's words. It was as if he'd been there when Jamie and Liz had finally talked. She'd come out with similar reasons for why she'd stayed so long.

He's obviously a wise man. And gentle. Kind. Sweet.

A few minutes later Stephen returned, carrying two mugs. He placed one on the nightstand and retook his seat. "Do you remember when you came with us on vacation to Florida, to stay at my grandma's place when she moved there?"

Jamie beamed. "That was a fantastic summer." They'd spent every day at the beach, and he'd come home with a great tan. It had been their last summer before the move to California.

"I was thinking about the jellyfish you kept finding on the beach." Stephen's eyes lit up. "And you in the pool. I could never keep up with you."

"I reckon I'd still give you a run for your money."

Stephen blinked. "You swim?" Then his face

fell. "I'm sorry. I keep doing this, don't I?"

Jamie speared him with a look. "You ever hear of something called the Paralympics? You know, athletes competing in sports, and all with disabilities?" He relented. "It's okay. You've had five minutes to get used to this, I get that. And you'd probably have a fit if you knew what I was considering doing this winter."

"What? Tell me."

Jamie grinned. "Skiing in Vermont. Wanna join me?" He threw out that last remark as a joke, but to his surprise, Stephen's face lit up.

"Seriously? I'd love to try that. I've always wanted to learn to ski."

Jamie stared at him. "We could do it. The snow sports program starts after Christmas. Want me to look into it?"

"Yeah. That sounds like a great idea." Stephen gave him a thoughtful look. "I guess I need to stop underestimating you, don't I?"

"*Now* you're getting it." Jamie grinned. "Does that mean you'll be up for paragliding too?" When Stephen's eyes widened and his mouth fell open, he laughed. "Maybe that's a step too far out of your comfort zone."

Stephen set his jaw. "Hey, anything *you* can do…"

Jamie burst out laughing. "*That's* the Stephen I remember. Dear Lord, the things I dared you to do…"

Stephen grimaced. "Yeah. Like eating a worm."

Jamie nodded. "I'm still amazed you did it."

"Well, if you could do it, so could I," Stephen retorted.

"Yeah, about that…" Jamie's cheeks warmed. "I didn't."

"Didn't what?"

"Eat a worm. I faked it. The worm ended up in my pocket."

Stephen glared at him. "I threw up because of you."

"How was I to know you'd really do it?"

"Duh. Because you *dared* me?" They stared at each other for a moment, and then both started laughing.

Jamie sagged into his pillows, content.

"So… are you thinking of taking part in the next Paralympics?" Stephen asked after sipping his hot chocolate.

He chuckled and flexed his arms. "There's good, and then there's world class. I think I fall into the former. But thanks for the compliment."

Stephen smiled. "Just trying not to underestimate you."

Jamie wrapped his hands around his mug. "You're clearly a fast learner." As he drank, he studied Stephen, thoughts flitting through his mind. It occurred to him that there was another theory to account for Stephen's wisdom—he'd known someone else in the same situation.

There is so much I don't know about you. Then he gave an internal shrug. They had plenty of time to learn everything about each other. There was a drawback to that, of course. Jamie wasn't sure how much of his personal life he was prepared to share with Stephen.

That was 'need-to-know' stuff, and Stephen

definitely did *not* need to know.

Then he realized Stephen was staring at his chest. "By the way," he said nonchalantly. "Any time you wanna come in here and watch me do my stretches, you're welcome." He grinned. "You don't even have to buy a ticket, and I'll reserve you a ringside seat."

Stephen snorted. "You always were an exhibitionist. Remember that time you dared me to run out with you into your back yard naked?"

"Yeah, and at the last minute you chickened out."

Stephen rolled his eyes. "It was daylight. Your mom was home."

Jamie stared at him. "That was all part of the excitement, dude. The thrill of getting caught. And she didn't catch me, did she?"

"No, but your neighbor across the way got an eyeful." Stephen cackled. "Well, not all *that* much of an eyeful, not with that little pea shooter of a dick."

Jamie couldn't resist. "It's gotten bigger since then." His heart pounded. "Wanna see?"

Stephen blinked, then smiled. "I think I'll pass."

Jamie waved his hand. "That's okay. I'll make sure to include it in my next stretching session. Gotta keep the spectators happy, right?" The image was right there in his head, him naked, his body taut as he stretched his hip flexors, his ass on show.

Stop that.

But one thought refused to budge.

What does your *dick look like now, Stephen?*

Chapter Ten

Jamie laid out his clothes on the bed. There was no way he'd go to his parents' party wearing sweats. He'd chosen a loose pair of jeans that thankfully had no trendy rips in them, and a dark blue shirt with a matching tie. His black shoes were polished and waiting for him on the dresser.

Then he caught the sound of running water.

Jamie wheeled furiously to the bathroom door and hammered on it. "Hey. You didn't say you were taking a shower."

"Did I need to?" Stephen hollered back. "I won't be long."

"Okay, new house rule. When we both need a shower, the disabled body has precedence over the able bodied." It took him longer than Stephen to get through his shower routine.

"Well, do you want me to stop showering so you can get in here, or am I allowed to finish first?"

It was on the tip of his tongue to say 'Well, we could always conserve water and shower together,' except he knew that was a nonstarter. *Quit thinking about what he looks like naked.*

"Doof." Jamie went back into his bedroom, acutely aware that Stephen was belting out Love On Top to piss him off. Then he smiled. *What do you know? Behind the shower curtain, we're all secretly Beyoncé.* He got on the bed to undress himself, doing his usual twist and roll to get his sweats off. Then he got into his chair, grabbed a towel from his closet and placed it on his lap.

Just in case. I wouldn't wanna give him a show. Except who'd want to look at his dick in its present state?

The water stopped, and Jamie headed back to the bathroom, in time to see Stephen emerge from it, a towel wrapped around his hips, revealing the fuzz on his belly that disappeared below the towel. His skin glistened with the water still beading on it. *Oh my God....*

Reality surpassed all his imaginings. Stephen was a vision of hotness.

Stephen grinned. "Happy now? I didn't even towel off. It's all yours." Then he went into his room and closed the door.

Jamie rolled into the bathroom and shut the door behind him. He got into the shower on autopilot, his thoughts still on the sight of Stephen in all his semi-naked glory. Stephen's chest was as hairy as his belly, and Jamie was a sucker for hair. His favorite porn site was of hairy guys, and he'd often fantasized about running his fingers through a guy's chest hair, tugging gently on it, or rubbing his face in it. He ached to know how it would feel.

Jamie looked down at his dick as he showered. "Well," he whispered, "if certain nerves were still attached, you'd be standing at attention right now." Who knew he had such a magnificent specimen sleeping in the next room?

There were times when it occurred to him that thinking about his best friend in such a carnal manner was wrong. Then he dismissed it. Thinking never hurt anyone. And what Stephen didn't know, wouldn't hurt him.

Why are all the best ones straight? Stephen had it all: he was smart, handsome, thoughtful... and sexy as fuck.

Stop that. Get showered. Party time, remember?

With a sigh, Jamie got on with the task of getting clean.

Jamie locked the car, and wheeled himself toward the sidewalk. Music drifted from the house, along with the sound of raised voices. He turned to Stephen with a smile. "There's still time to back out. We could go home and get takeout."

Stephen chuckled. "Again? And you know you wouldn't do that to your parents."

"Yeah, you're right. But do me a favor? If I tell you I've got a migraine, that's your cue to get me out of there, okay?" It wasn't like him to feel like this, but the prospect of a house full of well-meaning relatives and family friends filled him with dread. There was only so much sympathy he could stomach.

Stephen squeezed his shoulder. "You got it." Together they headed for the front door, which opened as they approached. Mom beamed when she saw Stephen.

"Oh my, look at you." She held her arms wide,

and Stephen got pulled into a hug he couldn't avoid, holding his flowers carefully. When she released him, she was still smiling. "I'm going to get a crick in my neck from looking up at you. Oh, and what lovely flowers. Thank you."

"It's great to see you again, Mrs. Lithgow."

Mom waved her hand. "Maureen. You're old enough to call me by my first name. Come on in."

"Does that include me too?" Jamie teased.

Mom rolled her eyes. "Idiot. Get in here."

Laughing, he followed them into the house. Mom went to put the flowers in water. The chatter and music grew louder as they neared the living room. Jamie paused at the threshold, took a deep breath, then wheeled himself across it.

Dad was standing near the door. He greeted him before shaking Stephen's hand vigorously. "So good to see you, my boy."

"You too, sir." Then Stephen was engulfed in an exuberant hug from Liz. He beamed at her. "Hey, look at you. The pretty fairy obviously paid you a visit," he joked.

Liz hit him on the arm. "Swine."

"When you've quite finished attacking our guest, why don't you get Stephen a drink?" Dad suggested. "Oh, and one for Jamie."

Jamie let out a gasp. "I see it all now. It was Stephen you wanted to come tonight. I was just the chauffeur."

Dad rolled his eyes. "You get *your* drink when you've said hello to some people who've been dying to meet you."

Jamie gave him a mock glare. "Oh, *I* get it.

Bribery, huh?" He gave the packed room a cursory glance. "This isn't going to work, Dad." There was no way he could get around that room, not without rolling over someone's toes.

Dad apparently came to the same conclusion. "There are fewer folks in the dining room. How about we put you in there, and guests can come see you?"

Jamie preened. "So I'm royalty and they're coming for an audience? Cool."

His dad laughed. "Trust you to see it like that. Well, right this way, your *Majesty*." He walked out of the living room and opened the door to the dining room. The connecting doors between the two rooms were already open, but Dad was correct—there were fewer people in there. Jamie wheeled himself to the corner and backed into it.

"This is fine," he said with a smile. Actually, it was more than fine, being tucked away like that. Then Mom came toward him, his Aunt Deborah in tow, and Jamie pasted on a smile. "Hey there. I haven't seen you in years."

Aunt Deborah's gaze stuttered down to his chair, and then she jerked her head up. "How are you?" Her voice dripped with sympathy.

"I'm great!" Jamie declared enthusiastically. "I've finished training for the Paralympic swimming team. It certainly keeps me in shape." He tried to keep a straight face.

Aunt Deborah blinked several times in quick succession. "That's Jamie's little joke," Mom said with a bright smile, before firing him a warning glare.

"Well, I did think you'd have said something if

he was doing that. He does look well, though."

It was on the tip of Jamie's tongue to say, '*He* is sitting right here, you know.'

"Jamie looks great," Stephen said as he joined them. He flashed Jamie a quick smile. "I bet you put a lot of guys at the gym to shame."

He gave Stephen a grateful glance as he handed Jamie a glass. "I try."

Stephen greeted Aunt Deborah with a polite smile. "Hi. I'm Stephen, Jamie's roommate, and once upon a time, his best friend."

Aunt Deborah nodded. "I think I remember you. Didn't you move to the west coast?"

"That was me." Stephen's eyes sparkled. "But now I'm back."

"Yeah, to bug me," Jamie added. Aunt Deborah made some noises about mingling, and walked away.

Mom glared at him again. "If I bring more people to see you, will you be nice?"

"I'll be me," Jamie said simply.

Mom sighed. "That's what I'm afraid of." She patted Stephen's arm, then left them.

Jamie let out a long breath. "Thanks for that. How would you like to be my bodyguard for the rest of the evening?"

"Sure, but in that case, we'll need supplies. And I saw some mozzarella sticks with cranberry dip that had your name all over them. Plus, they've got nachos."

Jamie placed his hand over his heart. "My hero." Stephen merely laughed and walked off in the direction of the kitchen. Within seconds, Liz and Phil joined Jamie.

He shook Phil's hand. "Good to see you again." He grinned. "How are you surviving your first family get-together?"

Phil groaned. "I've already been asked six times when me and Liz are going to announce the engagement."

Liz chuckled. "I told them we're gonna live in sin."

Jamie beamed. "That's my sis."

She knelt beside his chair and leaned in. "Oh, My. God. Didn't Stephen turn out well?" She fanned herself with her hand.

Phil glared. "Hey. I'm not sure I like my girlfriend ogling another guy."

She laughed. "That's not another guy—that's Stephen. He and Jamie grew up together." Then she whacked Phil on his leg. "And I can look, okay? If you can drool over Megan Fox every time she's on TV, I can appreciate that Stephen is a really good-looking guy." She glanced at Jamie and leaned in. "Is he taken?"

Jamie huffed. "I have no idea. He hasn't mentioned anyone in California." He took a sip of his drink. "We don't exactly discuss our personal lives."

"Well, I can understand why you wouldn't want to talk about *your* love life," Liz commented.

"Ha. What love life?"

"But I'm surprised you haven't asked Stephen about his." Her eyes sparkled. "Want me to? I can be subtle—unlike you."

"Hey," he said indignantly. "I can do subtle."

Liz snorted. "Yeah, right. Like that time you asked Mrs. Bercowitz next door if she needed a razor."

"I was twelve," Jamie protested. "I'd just asked Dad about shaving. *And* she had a mustache."

Phil burst into laughter, as Stephen walked toward them.

"What have I missed?"

"Jamie being Jamie, of course," Liz said with a chuckle. She went to pick up one of the mozzarella sticks he'd brought, but Stephen held them out of reach.

"Oh no you don't. Get your own. These are Jamie's and mine."

Jamie gave her a smug look. "See? *He's* loyal."

Stephen snickered. "No, *he* happens to share a house with you. I'm not stupid. I'm keeping you sweet." He pointed to the guests. "Now go mingle, like a good little hostess."

Liz narrowed her gaze. "God, it's like I'm a kid all over again. My *other* big brother is back."

"Ain't life grand?" Jamie said with a grin. He laughed as Liz tugged Phil away from them. Stephen handed him the plate of snacks, then dragged a chair over to place it next to his wheelchair. "Thanks, by the way."

"For feeding you?"

"No, for stepping in when Aunt Deborah was here."

"It was nothing. I figured you needed some support. Some *polite* support."

Jamie gave a mock gasp. "Are you implying I can't be polite?"

"Implying?" Stephen snorted. "Hell, I'm out and out *saying* it. If I let you speak your mind, you'd eviscerate her in a heartbeat. Verbally, of course." He looked into the packed living room. "Liz hasn't changed much."

Jamie smiled. "Still want her for a sister?"

He laughed. "Oh wow. I did say that, didn't I? She and Marie always got along so well."

Jamie caught sight of a vaguely familiar figure coming their way. "Uh-oh. Incoming." He straightened in his chair as a middle-aged man walked up to him, smiling.

"You probably don't remember me," the man began, speaking slowly and carefully. "I'm Wayne Ericsson. I work with your dad. The last time I saw you was at a party, oh, thirteen or fourteen years ago. Of course, that was before." He cleared his throat.

Jamie didn't have to ask what that meant. "I do recall you, Mr. Ericsson. You used to pull out your dentures and try to scare my sister." Which at the time he'd thought was a gross thing to do.

Mr. Ericsson blinked. "Wow. Fancy you being able to remember that." He glanced at Stephen. "I remember you too. David tells me you've moved in with Jamie. Well, I think that's admirable."

Stephen stilled. "I don't understand."

Jamie did. He gripped the arms of his chair.

"Why, you've done such a selfless thing. I'm sure Jamie appreciates you being around to help him. You must be such a comfort to him." Gone was Mr. Ericsson's slow, measured delivery. Apparently, Stephen could cope with normal speed.

Before Jamie could utter a word, Stephen stood, towering over him. "I think you've got things the wrong way round," he said quietly. "Jamie was kind enough to lend *me* a hand when I needed it. And he is *more* than capable of taking care of himself. He's been doing it without anyone's help for a good few years now."

Mr. Ericsson's face flushed. "Of course he has."

Stephen frowned. "You *can* talk to him directly, you know? I mean, he's sitting right here."

Mr. Ericsson swallowed. "It was good to see you again after all these years." And with that, he walked off.

"Sorry about that," Stephen murmured. "I tell you to be polite, and then I go and say something like that."

Jamie let go of the chair, reached for Stephen's hand, and squeezed it. "It's okay," he said in a low voice.

Stephen gazed at him in obvious bemusement. "How is it okay? First off, he talked to you like you were an imbecile. Then he acts like you're not even there."

"I'm used to people treating me like I'm part of the wallpaper," Jamie confessed. He patted the arm of the chair. "This is all they see, and with it come all kinds of preconceptions."

"In that case, I'm not moving from your side tonight." Stephen's eyes blazed. "And if anyone else tries that same crap, they'll have me to deal with."

Jamie smiled. "Looks like I picked the perfect bodyguard." He lifted the plate from his lap. "Have a mozzarella stick?"

Stephen glanced at it, then laughed. "You don't stay down for long, do you?"

"Nope. Pity parties are a waste of energy. I

prefer to dazzle folks with my intellect and wit. Let them see there's a mind here, not just a crippled body." Stephen's face tightened, and Jamie shook his head. "And that's not how *I* see myself, okay?"

At last Stephen smiled. "I rather like your intellect and wit." He leaned in. "Where's the bathroom? I need to go."

Jamie chuckled. "Down the hallway, next to the kitchen. Of course, *some* of us have an advantage."

"And what's that?"

Jamie gestured to his thigh. "I've got a bag taped to my thigh. I can go when I like."

Stephen laughed. "Smug bastard." And then he straightened. "Back in a sec."

Jamie watched him go, aware of the gorgeous body hiding beneath those tight jeans and black shirt. *Why did you have to be so... perfect?*

From across the room, Liz gave him a knowing smile, before walking over to him. She bent down and brought her lips to his ear. "Admit it. He's hot."

Damn her. "Okay. I'm not blind. He's hot." Then he glared at her. "And you shouldn't be thinking such things, Miss *I've Got A Boyfriend.*"

She straightened and grinned. "Like you said, I'm not blind." She sat in the chair Stephen had vacated. "You could always use him as bait."

He stared at her. "Excuse me?"

"You know, take him with you to a gay bar. You'd soon have lots of guys flocking to your table."

"Er, yes—to flirt with *him*. Besides, what makes you think he'd be up for being ogled by a bunch of gay guys?"

"It's only a suggestion." Liz's eyes gleamed.

"And remember what Dad used to say? 'Those that don't ask don't get.'" She kissed his cheek. "Think about it." Then she stood. "And now I'll go rescue Phil. I'm sure he knows all about Uncle Desmond's model trains by now." With a grin, she left him.

Jamie sighed. It was all very well telling him to ask Stephen. Jamie had the feeling that would be asking way too much.

Chapter Eleven

Stephen took the roasted vegetables out of the oven, and added to them the stir-fried pork strips with garlic, paprika and soy sauce. He hoped it would be okay. It was a new recipe, and Jamie was already making 'where are the Tums?' remarks.

Bastard.

He tossed the ingredients together, then piled them onto two warmed plates. "Come and get it," he hollered, knowing he'd have to go and bang on Jamie's door if Jamie was caught up in his work.

No response.

Stephen sighed and put the plates back into the oven. He went to Jamie's door and knocked. "Jamie? Dinner."

No response.

Stephen opened the door, and smiled. Jamie was asleep, his laptop open beside him on the comforter. Stephen walked over and stood by the bed, gazing at him.

He looks so young when he's sleeping. Not that he looked old when he was awake, but there were more lines to his face. Lines Stephen felt sure had been put there by his experiences. He fought the urge to stroke Jamie's cheek, not sure why he wanted to. It was as if Jamie's face invited touch. Instead, he touched Jamie's hand. "Hey. Sleepyhead."

Jamie opened his eyes. "Hey." He blinked.

Blinked again. "Was I asleep?"

"You were out of it." Stephen pointed to the laptop. "I think you've done enough for today. Dinner's ready."

Jamie smiled. "Great. Let me wash my face before I eat? It might wake me up."

"Sure." Stephen left him to it, and went into the kitchen to set the table. By the time he'd brought out the plates, Jamie was there, tucking his chair under and reaching for his fork.

"This smells wonderful."

Stephen chuckled. "Well, that's an improvement on asking where the Pepto-Bismol is." He sat at the table and tried a piece of pork. "Hey, this is okay."

"Don't sound so surprised. You're a good cook."

Stephen gazed at him incredulously. "Wow."

"What do you mean, wow?"

He smiled. "I've been living here for a month and that's the first time you haven't made a joke about my cooking."

Jamie became very still. "That makes me an asshole."

"I don't mind the jokes," Stephen protested. "I kind of assumed if you didn't like something, you'd tell me."

"Not complaining or saying nothing is *not* the same thing as paying a compliment. I should've said something before now." Jamie put down his fork. "Stephen, I love your cooking. There. I've said it."

Stephen chuckled. "Doof. Eat up."

They ate in silence for a while, but it was a

comfortable silence. When they were done, Jamie let out a contented sigh. "That was delicious. You can do that one again." He glanced toward the refrigerator. "Have we got any of that white wine left?"

"There's half a bottle. Why, do you want a glass?"

Jamie nodded, and Stephen got up from the table to fetch the glasses and the bottle.

"There's something I've been meaning to ask you for a while now, only I wasn't sure how to start."

Stephen paused, the refrigerator door open. "Uh-oh. Is that why you need alcohol?" he teased. "To give you Dutch courage?" He'd never heard Jamie sound so unsure of himself. "You can ask me anything. Of course, I may not answer *some* questions."

"When you left California…" Jamie stopped.

Stephen returned to the table with the wine. "Well, don't stop now. You've made a start." He poured the wine.

"Did you leave behind a string of women with broken hearts?"

And there they were, at the one topic Stephen had avoided since he'd moved in. "Why do you want to know?"

"Because we don't talk about stuff like this. I've wanted to ask for ages, only I didn't have the nerve."

"*You* didn't have the nerve? I may faint." Stephen took a long drink from his glass, his heartbeat speeding up a little.

"And you haven't answered the question."

There were no flies on Jamie.

He cleared his throat. "I can truthfully say, I've never broken a woman's heart."

Jamie's eyes widened. "Then one of them broke yours?"

His heart pounding, Stephen realized the moment of truth had arrived. "Okay... Here's an equation for you."

Jamie bit his lip. "Seriously? You're going with an *equation*?"

Stephen stared at him. "Let me tell it my way, or not at all."

Jamie mimed zipping his lips.

He started again. "I have never broken a woman's heart. A woman has never broken *my* heart. My heart has been broken, on more than one occasion. Ergo..." He met Jamie's gaze, his palms clammy. *Come on, Jamie. Do the math...*

Jamie frowned. "Okay, that doesn't make sen—" His eyes grew wider. "Oh. *Oh.*"

Stephen took another long drink.

"Are you telling me... what I *think* you're telling me?"

He took a deep breath. "If you think I'm telling you I'm gay, then yes." He waited for Jamie's first words.

What he didn't expect was Jamie's laughter.

It began as a chuckle, then grew, swelling into a peal of delighted laughter that went on and on, until Jamie's face was flushed and tears sparkled in his eyes.

"I didn't think it was *that* funny," Stephen said after a minute or two, affronted.

"That's because you haven't heard the

punchline yet," Jamie said, wiping his eyes.

"Oh? And what's the punchline?"

Jamie took a drink, then looked Stephen in the eye. "Me too."

It took a second or two for his meaning to sink in. Stephen gaped. "You're kidding." *No. Freaking. Way.*

Jamie shook his head.

"But... why haven't you said something before now?"

Jamie arched his eyebrows. "I could ask you the same question."

He'd come this far...

"Telling you I was gay meant owning up to a lot more, and I wasn't ready for that. I... I've not been lucky when it comes to romance." And wasn't *that* the understatement of the decade?

Jamie made a spluttering sound and started coughing. He put down his glass and covered his mouth with a tissue. Stephen watched anxiously for a moment, relieved when the coughing passed. Jamie sighed heavily. "And it's the same punchline again. Yet more things we have in common. Although you do surprise me."

"Why?"

Jamie gestured toward him. "Well, look at you! Even my sister thinks you're hot."

"Hot? Yeah right." Then Jamie's words hit home. "Liz thinks that?"

"Uh-huh. She even suggested I take you with me to a gay club, as a kind of guy magnet." He bit his lip. "I wasn't sure if you'd be comfortable with all the attention of a lot of gay men. To quote my mom, 'imagine that.'"

The irony…

"I think we have a lot to talk about." And Stephen was finally ready to talk, even though his stomach clenched at the prospect. His experiences made him look like a loser.

Jamie nodded. "Then how about we take the wine and go somewhere where I can get out of the chair, and we'll talk."

That meant Jamie's room. Stephen could do that.

Five minutes later, Jamie sat on his bed, supported by a mound of pillows, a glass of wine in his hand. "Who goes first?"

"I do." Stephen wanted to get the humiliation over with. He got comfortable on his side.

"Can I ask questions?"

He smiled. "Sure."

"When did you know? That you were gay, I mean."

Stephen took a drink before answering. "Sixteen. Of course, it took me two years to come out to Mom and Dad."

"How'd they take it?" Jamie's lips twitched. "I can see your mom freaking a little, that's all."

Stephen had to admit, Jamie really did have a handle on his parents. "They didn't go out and buy a bunch of pride flags to hang from the windows, that's for sure. Mom didn't come right out and say the word phase, but I'm pretty certain she was thinking it. They've gotten better with time, I have to say."

"And Marie?"

"She's had my back ever since."

Jamie nodded, smiling. "Which is why I loved your sister. She was awesome then, and it sounds like she still is."

"What about your parents?" He had a feeling Jamie's parents would have been a lot more supportive.

"Hey, you know me. I didn't wanna come right out and say 'Hey, I'm gay', so I thought I'd be a little… creative."

Stephen groaned. "What did you do?"

"When I was seventeen, I 'decorated' my bedroom. I had posters of Orlando Bloom, Wentworth Miller, Jesse Metcalfe, Jensen Ackles, Ashton Kutcher—"

"Wait. Hold the phone." Stephen stared at him. "You think Ashton Kutcher is *hot*?"

"Hey!" Jamie glared. "Okay, so he's not in the same league as Chris Evans or Jason Momoa, but he's pretty damn cute, all right? And this is *my* story, so shut up." He took a drink before continuing. "I covered my walls with my crushes. Then I got hold of a gay mag—nothing too raunchy—and cut out some of the sexiest guys, then stuck them all on a huge piece of paper, and put that on the wall. The finishing touch? I drew a lot of red hearts, cut 'em out, and then stuck them on my fave guys. Then I went to the mall. I didn't want to be around when Mom found them. I figured they'd be enough for her to get the picture."

"What happened?" Stephen would have loved to have been a fly on the wall.

"When I got home, Mom was in the kitchen. She took one look at me, then asked how I'd stuck all the posters on the walls, and she hoped they weren't gonna leave a mess."

"That was it?"

Jamie nodded. "Talk about an anticlimax. Then that weekend, Dad handed me a package. In it was a copy of The Joy of Gay Sex, and a box of condoms." He chuckled. "I wasn't expecting *that*. He said knowing how much I liked to figure things out, he thought I'd need an instruction manual, and this was the best he could come up with. And as for the condoms, he said 'Safety First.'"

"I fucking *love* your dad."

"Yeah." Jamie's brown eyes were warm. "I really lucked out with those two. Of course, Liz had a field day. Every time we went out somewhere after that, she was forever pointing out guys and saying 'Is he cute? Would you date him? How about that guy?'"

Stephen laughed. "That sounds like Liz. Did she really suggest taking me to a gay bar?"

"Oh yeah. She said you'd draw the guys to my table." He grinned. "Like bees to a honey pot."

That sobered him. "Trust me, you wouldn't want the kind of guys *I'd* attract."

Jamie cocked his head to one side. "Wanna explain that remark?"

Stephen drained his glass, coughing a little as the wine went down. He set his glass down with a sigh. "Every guy I ever dated turned out to be an asshole."

Jamie widened his eyes. "They can't *all* have been bad apples."

"Every last stinking one of them. We're talking humiliation, gaslighting, control freaks…"

"Did any of them ever… hurt you?" Jamie's

face tightened.

Stephen nodded. "I'm not going to talk about that, okay? It's enough that you know it happened. What made it worse was how difficult it was to break free."

Jamie let out a long breath. "Oh my God. *Now* it makes sense."

"What does?"

"All those things you said when I told you about Liz's abusive ex. I thought at the time how insightful your comments were. I had no idea you were speaking from experience."

Stephen poured what was left of the wine into his glass, and took a long drink. "So there you have it. Now you know why I'm a sad loser."

Jamie whacked him on the arm. "Hey. That's no way to talk about yourself."

"Why not? It's the truth, isn't it?"

"It's no way to talk to yourself either."

Stephen frowned. "Excuse me?"

Jamie sighed. "Look, we all talk to ourselves. And I don't mean the having a conversation out loud kind of talking. We tell ourselves stuff all the time. And that stuff *matters*. Hell, do you think I'd be where I am now if I'd kept telling myself life wasn't worth living? Because that was how I felt after the accident. That first year was... brutal. I didn't want to live, but at the same time I didn't want to die. I was just... numb. Waking up in that hospital bed every morning was like 'Dear Lord, so it *wasn't* a nightmare. It's fucking *real*.' And God, how it sucked to feel like that. But I couldn't keep on feeling like that, so I changed how I talked to myself. I told myself I was a survivor. That I was more than just my legs. That if my future was going to be in that fucking chair, then I'd accept it and be the best fucking Jamie Lithgow I could be."

"But I'm not *you*," Stephen cried out.

Jamie looked him in the eye. "No, you're not. You're Stephen Taylor, my best friend, awesome accountant—because hey, *someone* has to be, right?—and beautiful human being." He held his arm wide. "Come here."

Stephen blinked. "We're going to hug?"

Jamie's eyes were fire. "You're damn straight we're gonna hug. Because if I can't hug my best friend when he needs it, then what kind of friend am I? Now get your butt over here and let me hug you."

Stephen shifted across the bed, and Jamie put his arm around him. Stephen laid his head on Jamie's chest, listening to the reassuring beat of his heart.

"It's gonna be okay," Jamie said softly. "You gotta look on the bright side more often."

"There's a bright side?"

Jamie's chuckle reverberated through him. "Sure there is. Your best friend turned out to be gay. Ain't life grand?"

Stephen smiled against Jamie's chest. "You know, there *were* signs, only I wasn't paying attention."

"What signs?"

"Oh, things you said. Like how your neighbor makes the place look pretty. I should've put two and two together." He craned his neck to look up at Jamie. "But you didn't finish your story. How come you've not been lucky in love either?"

Jamie didn't say a word but pointed to the chair.

Stephen's heart went out to his friend. "Then they're blind and stupid, not to see how amazing you are." He lowered his head, loving the feel of Jamie's strong arm around him. It had been a long time since someone had held him, and the best part was Stephen knew he was safe.

Jamie would never hurt him.

"Wanna watch a movie?"

Stephen smiled. "Better make it a comedy. I think I need to laugh right now." To his surprise, Jamie kissed the top of his head. Stephen sat up and stared at him. "What was that for?"

Jamie's eyes shone with that same warmth. "I figured you needed it." He cocked his head to one side. "Was I wrong?"

"No, you weren't wrong," Stephen admitted.

It had been the perfect way to end their conversation.

K.C. Wells

Chapter Twelve

Jamie switched off the TV around eleven, when soft snores came from the other side of the bed. He rolled onto his side and gazed at the sleeping Stephen.

The *gay* Stephen.

Well, what do you know about that? Maybe there is *a God after all.*

He couldn't deny how much it had pained him to hear about Stephen's past relationships. The idea of someone hurting him... Then it struck him that he knew exactly how Stephen had felt about the drunken bastard who'd gotten behind the wheel of his car. Jamie wanted to get his hands on the fuckers who would abuse someone they claimed to love. Except he had no idea if Stephen had been in love with those guys, or vice versa.

Was I *looking for love when I went to gay bars, or a hookup?* If he were brutally honest, going back a few years, a night of hot, dirty sex would have been enough. Not that he got even close to getting that.

And now?

Now he'd take what he could get. Although if Mr. Right turned up in the meantime... Except the 'taking what he could get' part? That was a lie. He was holding out for Mr. Right, pure and simple. Because after all those first dates that never went any further, he damn well deserved something special.

Stephen stirred in his sleep, and Jamie snapped

back from his musing to stare at his handsome face. It would only take a slight shake to waken him and send him on his way to his own bed. Jamie smiled to himself. *Of course, I could wake him with a kiss...* Because those soft-looking lips were crying out to be kissed.

And who says he wants *me to kiss him?*

With a sigh he gave Stephen a gentle nudge. Those blue-green eyes blinked, and Stephen rubbed them. "Did the movie finish?"

Jamie laughed quietly. "No. It got a little difficult to hear it over the added sound effects, that's all."

He flushed. "Aw, crap. I'm sorry."

"It's late anyway, and you've got work tomorrow. Go get comfortable in your own bed."

Stephen smiled. "I don't know. Yours is pretty comfy." He got up off the bed. "Sleep well."

"You too." As an afterthought, Jamie added, "Sweet dreams."

Stephen left the room, closing the door behind him.

Jamie rolled onto his back, staring at the ceiling. *So what if he's gay? That doesn't change anything, does it?* Except to make him feel slightly less guilty about the whole wanting to see Stephen naked thing.

On the nightstand his phone buzzed, and he reached for it.

You awake? Can we talk?

Jamie smiled and clicked on Call. "Since when do you ever message me this late?"

Liz laughed. "I've been on a date. I just got back."

"And you thought you'd wake me up? How sweet. By the way, if you're calling to share intimate details of your love life, the next time I see you? I'm gonna run you over with my chair."

"I'm calling to find out if you asked him yet."

Jamie frowned. "I feel like I'm watching a movie where they skipped several pages of the script. Asked who what?"

"Idiot. Did you ask Stephen if he'd go with you as date-bait?"

Jamie snorted. "Did you just invent that?"

"Yes. Now answer the question."

He sighed. "No, I didn't ask him, because something important happened before I could."

"Like what?"

"Well… for one thing, I found out he's gay." When silence fell, Jamie checked the phone, but they were still connected. "Liz? You there?"

"Oh my God, that's wonderful!"

"What's got you all worked up?" He couldn't miss the elation.

"You and Stephen. You would be perfect for each other."

Bless her naive little heart.

"Wait, you think we should date each other because we both happen to be gay? It doesn't work that way, sis." Though God knew he'd love it if it did.

"But it could," she said decisively. "Are you telling me you're not attracted to him? Because say that and I'll call bullshit. I saw how you looked at him at the party."

"And how was that exactly?"

Liz snorted. "I'm amazed no one tripped over

your tongue on the floor, the way you were drooling over him."

"That's because he's gorgeous. And yes, I thought he was gorgeous even when I thought he was straight."

"See?" Lord, she sounded like she was about to hyperventilate.

"Liz. Calm down a sec, and listen to me." Jamie hated to burst her bubble, but it was time for a dose of reality. "Stephen is my best friend, okay? And that's exactly how he sees me."

"Do you know that for certain?"

Okay, she had him there. "No, of course I don't. Talented as I am, mind reading is *not* one of my gifts."

"So how do you know how he feels about you? For all you know, he could be lying in bed right this second, jerking off to thoughts of you."

Jamie gave a mock gasp. "And I used to think you were a lady."

Liz cackled. "Sucker. Now tell me what you're going to do next."

From beyond his bedroom door, he caught the sound of the toilet flushing. "Now? I'm going to go to the bathroom, seeing as Stephen is done with it for the night."

"But you *know* I'm right," she wailed.

Jamie sighed again. "Okay, I'll be honest. I would love it if something developed between me and Stephen, okay? But I am *not* gonna push it to make things happen. You know the saying, it takes two to tango?"

"So you won't make a move unless he does? And what if he doesn't? What if—God forbid—he's waiting on *you* to do exactly the same thing?"

"And what if you let me go do my ablutions and get some beauty sleep? Because he sure isn't gonna look twice at me if I've got dark circles under my bloodshot eyes."

There was a pause. "What are you afraid of?"

Damn her for seeing right through him as usual.

Jamie swallowed. "What if... what if he's like all the rest?" He didn't think he could take it if Stephen proved to be as blinkered as everyone else Jamie had ever been interested in.

"He couldn't be."

God, he loved her optimism. It rivaled his own at times.

"Why not? He's human, like all the other guys I was interested in."

"Yes, but he *knows* you better than any of them."

"He knew me before the accident. I've changed. For that matter, so has he." God, they could talk about it until the cows came home, and he'd still be none the wiser. "Go to bed, sis."

"Okay. Love you."

That brought him a smile. "Love you too. We'll talk more this weekend, okay?"

"Okay." Another pause. "Sweet dreams of Stephen."

He chuckled. "You couldn't resist, could you?" And with that, he disconnected.

Jamie transferred into his chair and headed for the bathroom, his mind in a mess.

It doesn't matter what I want. He has to want it too. And unless Stephen was an exceptional man,

Jamie's wheelchair was going to be an insurmountable obstacle.

Again.

Stephen went into the small kitchen that served the office, and poured himself a cup of coffee. His lunch break was almost over. He greeted the three accountants who were standing around, chatting.

Stephen liked the atmosphere in the office. They weren't a big operation by anyone's standards, but there was already a family feel to the enterprise. New business kept rolling in, and if things continued in this vein, they'd have to take on new staff.

Way to go, Dad.

He knew how nervous his dad had been about the whole venture, but that hadn't held him back. As for Stephen's concerns about working with him, reality was nothing like he'd anticipated. They worked well together—when they saw each other. Stephen oversaw the day-to-day running of the company, and Dad left him to it. Their paths usually crossed a couple times a day, though sometimes not at all.

This is going to work out.

He walked back to his office and closed the door. Through the window, the Boston skyline was visible, with its glittering skyscrapers that reflected the sky like mirrors. There might not have been as much sunshine as there was in San Diego, but Stephen couldn't care less. He was happy to be back.

He turned his head at the firm knock. "Come in." He smiled when his dad entered. "Since when do *you* need to knock? It's your company."

Dad shrugged. "But it's *your* office." He cocked his head to one side. "You got a minute?" He closed the door behind him.

"For you? Several." Stephen gestured to the chair facing his desk. "Please, sit." He waited until his dad was seated. "Is everything okay?" Such a visit was far enough out of the ordinary to have him concerned.

"I wanted to talk to you, if that's okay."

Stephen's scalp prickled. "Sure." He sat in his chair, his hands around his cup.

Dad studied him for a moment, and something quivered in Stephen's stomach. At last Dad spoke. "Are you happy?"

Stephen blinked. "Sir?"

"I may be wrong, but I got the feeling you weren't all that happy in California. Not that you ever said as much…"

Stephen chuckled. "We don't talk about personal stuff, remember? The whole conversation that went something like, 'I know what goes on, but I don't *want* to know, if you catch my drift.'"

"Yeah. I wasn't going to win any prizes for The World's Best Dad, was I? You kind of threw us for a loop there." He chuckled too. "You know, your mom blamed it on us moving to California."

Stephen gaped at him. "She thought California made me gay?"

"Yeah, I know how it sounds." He paused,

before looking Stephen in the eye. "But I got the feeling now and then that there were things going on that I needed to know about."

Stephen repressed a shiver. "Trust me. You didn't."

Dad narrowed his gaze. "But you *are* happy with the move? To be working with me?"

"Of course." If his dad had to ask, then Stephen was doing something wrong.

Dad nodded, apparently satisfied with his response. "Good. I'm glad." He gave a sweep of his arm. "Because all this is for you."

"Sir?" He frowned.

Dad leaned back in his chair. "Son, I'm fifty-five. Do you really think I want to be running a company for the next twenty years? I started this business because I was sick and tired of working for someone else. Making someone else's dreams come true. We're going to work hard and make this a great company. And then? I'll hand the reins over to you, and I'll sit back and retire. Once I'm gone, it'll be yours. So it matters to me that you're happy in your work."

Stephen smiled. "I am. But can we not talk about something that's a long way off yet?"

Dad laughed. "We're all gonna die sometime, son. It was important to me to make sure you'll be provided for. Now I guess all we have to do is get the rest of your life sorted out. A home. A partner."

Stephen arched his eyebrows. "You're going to find me a partner too?"

Dad snorted. "I figure I'll leave that part up to you." He paused. "I know your mom and I don't talk about such things, but we do think about them. A lot. We want you to be happy."

Warmth flooded through him. "I want that too."

Dad gave him another keen look. "You would tell us, wouldn't you? If there was anything wrong?"

"Dad, there's nothing wrong," Stephen assured him. "I love sharing a place with Jamie. I love my work. And… I love that we've talked. It's only taken us *how* many years to do it?"

"I know." His dad's face flushed. "And I'm glad we've talked too. Only…"

Stephen held up his hand. "I get it. There are still things you don't want to know about. That's fine, because there's stuff I don't want to share."

His dad let out a huge breath, his relief evident. "So it's really working out? You and Jamie sharing?"

Stephen smiled. "Yeah. I got my best friend back."

"Except he's not quite the same."

He met Dad's gaze. "In all the ways that matter, he is." His phone gave a quick buzz. "And that's my alarm to say lunch is over, so I guess I'd better get back to running your company." He grinned. "Got to make sure you've got enough money to make your retirement comfortable—and Mom happy, of course."

"I'm not ready to sit back just yet."

Stephen laughed. "Glad to hear it." Dad got up and left his office, and Stephen finished his coffee.

I didn't see that *coming.*

The only thing that pained him about the conversation was the reference to Jamie's situation. It looked like Jamie was right. Some people had a lot of preconceptions about the disabled.

Stephen hadn't expected his dad to be one of them.

Chapter Thirteen

October

Jamie finished loading the dishwasher. It had been his turn to make dinner, and his pasta with a spicy tomato sauce had been simple but apparently well received: Stephen had eaten two helpings. Which gave Jamie all the ammunition he needed.

"Dude, you wanna watch it, you know." Jamie dropped his gaze to Stephen's middle. "The way you eat? You're gonna pile on the pounds *so* freaking fast."

Stephen patted his belly. "You see any flab? No, you don't. You know why? Because I do sit-ups every single night."

Jamie nodded in approval. "You ever think about coming with me to the gym? It'd be fun to work out together."

Stephen gave him a thoughtful glance. "Yeah, but when? I don't get home until after six. Then we eat, we veg out, and before you know it, it's time for bed."

"Then let's go when you get home. I'm not saying we need to spend hours there. For God's sake, my gym is right around the corner. I don't even take my car." He batted his eyelashes. "What do you say?"

Stephen laughed. "My God. You *still* do that."

Jamie laughed. "Aha. I sense you're weakening."

"Sure. We'll go tomorrow." Stephen smiled. "So what if it's Friday night? It's not like either of us has a hot date, right? Is it usually busy?"

"I've no idea what it's like at that time. I normally go earlier. But I should think everyone has the same idea as you, and they're off doing better things with their Friday nights." He smiled. "If he's there, I'll introduce you to a friend of mine, Jack. His body puts both of us to shame. Even his muscles have muscles."

Stephen's eyes twinkled. "Aha. *Now* I understand why you like going there."

"Not so fast with the assumptions. Jack is straight and married. And believe it or not, I don't go there on the hunt for guys."

"So you say." That twinkle was still there.

Jamie wasn't about to share some of his gym encounters. At times it was as if he'd grown a second head, judging by the looks he got. "I don't shower there. I come home for that." The gym provided a disabled access shower, but it shared a space with the cleaning products, mops, and buckets. He felt more comfortable in his own bathroom.

Stephen gestured to the wine bottle. "Do you want any more of that?"

Jamie shook his head. "I'm good." He waited until Stephen had put the bottle away in the refrigerator. "I *will* have a coffee, however."

"I'll make a fresh pot." Stephen went about his task. Once the coffee was on, he put away yesterday's now clean dishes he'd taken from the dishwasher, and wiped down the surfaces. Jamie liked how domesticated he was.

Stephen glanced over at him. "What are you smiling about?"

"I was thinking. My first roommate, and I didn't have to house-train you."

Stephen rolled his eyes. "Thank God those years in college were useful for something."

Jamie laughed. "Hey, that's pretty good. You're learning."

"Well, look who I have for a teacher," he retorted.

"Speaking of teachers…. You remember Mr. Wilson, our history teacher in seventh grade?"

Stephen stilled. "Tall, skinny, always wore jeans and a sweater?"

"That's the one. Well, shortly after you left, he got married."

Stephen frowned. "So what? He wasn't *that* bad looking." He grinned. "In fact, if I remember rightly, he was kinda cute."

Jamie matched his grin. "Evidently his *husband* thought so too."

Stephen gaped. "No freaking *way*."

Jamie nodded gleefully. "It was the talk of the school district, apparently."

"Hey, they didn't try to fire him, did they?"

Jamie snorted. "As if they could. His uncle was the School Superintendent."

"How do you know all this?"

He buffed his fingernails on his shirt. "I had my sources. Well, one source, to be exact. A guy called Reece, whose mom was on the school board." When Stephen's brow furrowed, Jamie gave a wave. "He was after your time." And there was a whole lot more

Jamie could have said about Reece if he felt so inclined.

"So what was Mr. Wilson's husband like? Did you ever see him?"

"A couple of times, sure. I saw them together at the mall one Saturday. They were shopping for clothes." He sighed. "They held hands when they thought no one could see. I loved that." He cocked his head to one side. "What was high school like over on the West coast? I keep imagining beautiful teenagers with perfect teeth, tans, and a Californian drawl."

Stephen chuckled. "You nailed it. We're talking 90% drop-dead gorgeous. So many of the girls came to school with perfect hair and make-up every day, they could've been models instead of students."

"And what about the guys?"

"Most of them were pretty much drop-dead gorgeous too."

"And were any of them gay?" It was Jamie's roundabout way of finding out if Stephen had had any crushes he didn't mind talking about.

Stephen joined him at the table with two mugs of coffee, and sat. "Seeing as one of them was my first, I sure hope so."

Jamie grinned. "Do tell."

Stephen waved a hand. "You don't want to hear this."

"Oh, but I do. And I'll make you a deal. Tell me yours, and then I'll tell you mine."

"Fine." Stephen leaned back. "His name was Corbin."

"Gimme details. Blond, redhead, brunette? Height, weight, shoe size, sexual preferences?"

Stephen laughed. "How about you let me talk without interrupting me?" Jamie zipped his lips, and he continued. "He was six-two, with blond hair, blue eyes, golden tan, and yup, a perfect white smile."

"He sounds like a perfect dreamboat, as your mom said once."

Stephen groaned. "Oh God. She was talking about Patrick Stewart in X-Men, wasn't she?"

"Didn't she say the same thing about Yul Brynner in The Magnificent Seven?" Jamie waggled his eyebrows. "Got a thing for baldies, huh? Does your dad know? Does he realize one of these days he's gonna wake up with a shaved head? Hide the razors and clippers." Stephen whacked him on the arm, and he rubbed it briskly. "Ow. Go easy. Now *my* idea of a dreamboat in that movie? Hugh Jackman."

"Yours, and about one million other gay men's," Stephen said with a grin.

"Let's get back to Corbin." Jamie widened his eyes. "He was taller than you? Way to go. Because I really can't visualize you with a five-feet nothing guy. Although I suppose that would work too. He could stand straight and blow you at the same time." Stephen squinted at him, and Jamie shut up quickly.

"It was almost the summer, the end of high school. His parents went away for a weekend, and he threw a party. I think most of the senior year turned up. Anyhow, when it got near midnight, and everyone started leaving, he asked me to stay."

Jamie hoped to God Stephen's first time had been good. "Was it okay?"

Stephen snickered. "It was short. We lasted about five minutes, and then his grandparents came by. Turned out his parents had asked them to keep an eye on the place. They'd been to the theater and were stopping by to check on him."

"Oh no! Did you get caught?"

"No, but that was only because he had me climb out of his bedroom window and shimmy down the tree." Stephen snorted. "I damn near broke my ankle when I fell. Had to tell Mom and Dad I tripped on the way home. Thankfully, they believed me."

"Did you at least get a replay?"

"Nope. The near miss was enough to cool his jets. Not that I saw him again after graduation. To be honest, I was surprised as hell when he asked me to stay that night. He'd been giving me the eye all through the party, but I never expected it to come to anything. We moved in different circles, so to speak." Stephen sighed. "He probably thought I'd be a sure thing. Which I was. I couldn't wait to get laid." He peered at Jamie. "What about you?"

Jamie snorted. "You're not gonna believe this. My first time didn't last that much longer than yours. I was on a field trip my senior year. They took us to a national park. Anyhow, I snuck off with Reece when we figured no one was looking, and we hid out in the woods."

"Reece? The one whose mom is on the school board?" Stephen laughed. "Did Mommy know what her little boy was up to?"

Jamie gave a loud snort. "He sure wasn't little."

"So what was he like?"

"Nothing like Mr. Greek God Corbin, I can tell you that. Reece was a bit of a nerd, but *man*, he sure could kiss. I guess that was when I found out I could kiss too, because I steamed up his glasses."

Stephen laughed. "Sounds like it was a memorable experience."

Jamie nodded. "And it taught me something too."

"I dread to ask."

He grinned. "Never fuck up against a tree. That bark is *rough*. My ass was scratched to hell. Thank God it didn't last that long." He sighed. "Actually, it was over way too fast, because we didn't want anyone to notice we were gone. I was his first too. We managed enough time for a BJ and a couple minutes of inexpert fucking. His hands were *everywhere*. So we popped each other's cherries—well, Reece got his first blow job at least—and then we rejoined the group." He snickered. "With me doing my best to walk like I hadn't had Reece's nine incher wedged up my butt."

Stephen winced. "Ouch. Yup, that definitely sounds memorable." Then he stared at Jamie with wide eyes. "Dear Lord, tell me you guys had lube."

Jamie snorted. "Are you kidding? As if either of us was about to walk into a drugstore and buy lube."

"Then I repeat. *Ouch*."

"It's not as bad as it sounds. We made do with… something else." He coughed.

Stephen bit his lip. "Oh God. What did you use?"

Jamie felt sure his cheeks were bright red. "We brought bag lunches, and Reece's mom packed him a bologna sandwich, and.." He clammed up. He'd already said *way* too much.

Stephen cocked his head. Then a moment later

his eyes were wider than ever. "You… you used *mayo* as lube?"

"It was all we had! And if you think *your* mom is a hard ass about neatness… Imagine trying to explain mayo stains in your underwear."

Stephen burst into laughter, tears trickling down his cheeks, and Jamie couldn't help himself. A second later, he was laughing too. Stephen finally got himself under control. "So what did you tell her?"

Jamie gave him an incredulous stare. "Dude, *really*? I buried them so deep in the garbage, they'd *never* be seen again. How stupid do you think I am?"

He shook his head, chuckling. "Well, apart from the mayo, it sounds like we had similar experiences. Thank God sex got better."

Jamie kept silent on that one. In fact, he wanted to change the subject in case Stephen asked any awkward questions that Jamie didn't want to answer.

"You know, there's something else our experiences had in common," Stephen announced suddenly, his expression more serious.

"And what's that?"

"Well, I don't know about you and Reece, but I didn't love Corbin. Which was kind of sad. I always told myself my first time would be with someone I loved, but when it came down to it…"

"You wanted to know if sex was anything like it was in your head, and he was right there, offering to help you find out." When Stephen nodded slowly, Jamie sighed. "Yeah. I'd wished for the same thing."

And if it had been you? I think I'd have gotten my wish.

He couldn't talk about this anymore. They were

sailing way too close to the wind, and Jamie didn't want to blurt out something he'd later regret.

Like how he *really* felt about his roommate.

"Hey, isn't it your mom's birthday coming up real soon?"

Stephen nodded. "Saturday. Fancy you remembering that."

"I told you. I forget nothing. So what have you got planned for her?"

"You know, the usual. A card, flowers…"

Jamie sighed heavily. "Sure. Because nothing says 'I couldn't be bothered' more than a bunch of flowers you grabbed on the way to see her. Why not make an effort? Surprise the hell out of her?"

"Why—you got an idea of how I could do that?"

"Of course." Jamie beamed. "Bake her a cake."

Stephen stared at him. "I can cook, sure, but I can't bake."

"You can follow a recipe, can't you?"

He blinked. "Well, yeah."

"So what's different about baking? You just follow the recipe."

Stephen gave him a speculative glance. "Can *you* bake?"

Jamie shrugged. "I have no idea. I've never tried. But how difficult can it be?"

That got him a grin. "In that case, *you're* going to help me."

It was then that Jamie regretted saying anything. He got a really bad feeling about this.

"You still think I should bake her a cake?" Stephen asked, his eyes sparkling with humor. "Because you're looking less enthusiastic by the second."

Jamie thought back to all those times he'd watched Mom in the kitchen, weighing flour, cracking eggs, whisking, beating, folding… "Nah, we can do this."

How difficult could it be?

Chapter Fourteen

Jamie had been right about one thing—there weren't many people at the gym the following evening.

"This looks like a good place," Stephen commented as they stepped onto the main floor.

"That's because it *is* good." Jamie had found it not long after he'd bought the house. He had no experience with gyms, but from what Jack told him, this one was better than most. For one thing, there was an elevator, not to mention a ramp at the main entrance. There was plenty of space between the machines for him to maneuver the chair. It wasn't until he'd been friends with Jack for a while that Jack confided in him. Apparently, when he'd first joined, all the exercise equipment had been placed a lot closer together. Jack had been looking for a gym for his wife, and he got to talking with the gym manager. Between them, they redesigned the layout, allowing for wheelchair access.

Not that Jamie had ever seen anyone else in a chair using the gym. Which was probably why he got as many glances as he did.

"Do you have a routine?" Stephen asked.

Jamie nodded. "I have a set of machines I like to use for chest, back and arms." He gestured to the array of machines on the left. "These are all upper body workout machines. On the other side, it's all lower body." He grinned. "Now what did you want to work on today?"

Stephen gazed at the machines. "Lower body, I think." He glanced down at his body. "Do you think I need to work on my legs?"

Shit. Jamie figured telling Stephen his legs looked pretty damn perfect was not the right response. "It's a good place to start," he offered.

"Yeah, but which machine do I start with?"

"Well, I'm not much help to you with those, but I spy a man who is." He waved at Carlos, who was wiping down the hip adduction machine. Jamie beckoned him over. "Hey, Carlos."

Carlos clasped hands with him briefly. "What you doin' here? This ain't your usual time."

"Well, you know what they say. A change is as good as a rest." Jamie pointed to Stephen. "This is my best friend, Stephen. I'm trying to get him to become a member. Would you talk him through the lower body stuff so he can have a go?" He winked. "You know, dazzle him?"

Carlos grinned. "I'll do my best to impress. So don't you be hovering. Go do your thing. The Seated Row is empty, and I know you like to start with that." He patted Stephen's arm. "I'll take good care of him."

"Good enough." Jamie glanced at Stephen. "Now, I will say this once. Don't overdo it. You hear? Just do a couple of sets on each one, okay?"

Stephen rolled his eyes. "Sure thing—*Dad.*" Carlos snickered at that, before leading him toward the Seated Leg Press.

Jamie headed for the Seated Row, his favorite. He positioned the chair as close to the padded seat as he could then transferred across, lifting his leg to sit astride it. The chest pad snug against his sternum, he leaned forward to grasp the grips and proceeded to slowly pull them toward his body. Across the way, Stephen was positioned on the sliding seat of the machine, his feet at chest height. Jamie took a moment to admire the curve of his calves and the toned look of his quads as he pushed with his feet, the seat sliding up and down with each motion.

The shorts were a definite bonus.

I could get to like buddying up at the gym. Especially if Stephen turned up in those shorts.

Jamie gave himself a mental kicking. *He came here to exercise, not so I could perv on him.* But *man*, he was easy on the eye. *It's those long legs.* Jamie kept imagining them flexing as Stephen crouched over him, squatting as he took Jamie's—

Nope. Nope. Nope. Stop that.

Jamie focused on his breathing, keeping his movements smooth. Except his gaze was drawn continually to Stephen. Then he noticed Carlos was showing him the V-Squat.

Oh no. Hell no.

Jamie lowered his gaze and did his utmost not to look, but it was no use. He had to see. He glanced across, and—

Sweet Jesus, look *at that ass.*

Jamie watched, entranced, as Stephen slowly went down into a squat, the padded rests on his shoulders, his ass tightly encased in those sinfully short shorts.

And what an ass. It didn't take much imagination to picture it naked, Jamie's hands on those firm cheeks, squeezing them, spreading them, baring him to Jamie's view.

Okay, who turned up the heat in here?

It was then that the thought occurred to him.

That fucker. He's doing this on purpose.

Except how could he? Stephen was looking in the opposite direction. And maybe that was what Jamie needed to be doing, because Stephen's bod was one hell of a distraction.

He finished up on the Row, then got back into his chair and headed for the Arm Curls machine. The choice was deliberate—it faced away from Stephen. Jamie rested his arms on the padded surface, and slowly curled them up toward his face, concentrating on his breathing.

Normality resumed.

Carlos appeared at his side. "Your friend is getting a lotta looks," he said with a grin.

"Oh?" Jamie kept his tone casual, his focus on his triceps.

"You think you can get him to join? Because he sure makes the place look nice."

Jamie stared at him. "I'll be sure to pass that on." He couldn't resist a little poke. "Especially to Ray."

Carlos's eyes widened. "You wouldn't."

No, he wouldn't dream of ratting on Carlos to his boyfriend, but Lord, it was fun yanking his chain. "I won't say a word," he promised. "But you'd better go clean up."

"What needs cleaning?"

"The floor. It's covered with your drool." Jamie chuckled. "And it sounds like you're not the only one."

"Yeah, but he don't even notice."

That stopped him dead in his tracks. "Seriously?" Jamie twisted around to see Stephen focused on his exercise, apparently oblivious to the appreciative glances he was getting from two or three of the gym members.

A wicked thought crossed his mind. *I bet I can make him notice* me.

This time when that small voice inside his head said he shouldn't be doing it, Jamie told it where to go.

Stephen had the sneaking suspicion he was going to regret this by the end of the day. Jamie's advice about a couple of sets had gone unheeded as he'd pushed himself, enjoying the physical exertion. He was really feeling some of those stretches, especially his inner thighs after that hip adduction machine.

He paused for a minute, searching for Carlos so he could move onto another machine, but Carlos was occupied, talking with a couple of guys at the far end of the floor. Stephen glanced around to find Jamie, and soon spotted the chair. Jamie had his back to him, pulling down on grips, his back flexed.

God, he was beautiful, his body moving sinuously.

How come I never noticed this before?

Then he reasoned he'd never seen Jamie without clothes, except for a brief glimpse that time as he was leaving the bathroom and Jamie was heading in. Judging by what he was seeing, he'd definitely missed out. Jamie's upper body was toned, not overly muscular, but with enough definition that Stephen wanted to trace over Jamie's skin with his tongue.

The impulse shocked him into stillness. He'd always thought of Jamie as, well, *Jamie*, his best friend, kind, generous and funny. The sort of man Stephen had yearned to meet and fall in love with. Someone solid and dependable. So it came as a bit of a shock to realize how much Stephen wanted him.

But I can't have him, can I? At least, not like that.

God, what a waste. Jamie deserved to be touched, caressed, kissed… Stephen stared at the wheelchair. *And because of that contraption, he's going to miss out on so much.*

It wasn't fair.

"Stephen?"

With a jolt, Stephen snapped back into the moment. Jamie was staring at him, smirking. "Contemplating your next move?"

Stephen laughed. "And I suppose you never zone out."

Jamie chuckled. "Not in the middle of the gym, no." His eyes gleamed. "Not overdoing it, are we?"

"No, *we're* not," he lied. If Jamie had said right then and there that they'd call it a night, he'd have willingly gone along. Not that he'd let Jamie know that. "I'm waiting for Carlos to talk me through the next machine."

"Okay. But remember what I said." Jamie wheeled himself over to another machine, just as Carlos approached, pointing to the next fiendish torture device.

Yeah. He'd overdone it already.

Jamie sat on his chair in the tub, letting the hot water sluice away his sweat and aches. Once he'd gotten focused, it had been a good workout. In fact, he'd done more than usual, but that was down to Stephen. In the latter half of their hour at the gym, it had become a sort of competition. If Jamie did two sets on a machine, Stephen did three. Jamie had laughed at that. It was like they were kids all over again.

Except kids didn't ache like a bastard after an hour's exercise.

He still felt it was a miracle he'd managed to work out at all, given the... distractions. *It wasn't wrong, was it, to be lusting after my roommate?* It wasn't as if Jamie was about to jump on Stephen's bones. But Lord, the thought of doing that sent heat pulsing through him.

He switched off the water and reached for his towel. At least Stephen wasn't waiting outside. He'd showered at the gym. Jamie dried his hair vigorously, then toweled himself as much as he could before transferring into his chair. As he opened the door, he caught the unmistakable sound of a low groan.

"Are you okay?"

A sigh followed. "Yeah. This is what I get for not following advice. I'm my own worst enemy."

"Gimme a sec. I need to put on some clothes." Jamie rolled into his bedroom, got onto his bed, and did his usual rock and roll routine to get into them. When he was decent, he went into the living room. Stephen was stretched out on the couch.

"I'm dying," he announced.

Dear Lord, that's so cute.

Jamie snorted. "That bad, huh?" He wheeled himself up to the couch. "Where does it hurt?"

"My legs. My butt."

"Well, I can help with your legs. As for your butt, you can deal with that." Not that he didn't love the idea of digging his thumbs into that firm ass and kneading it.

Down boy.

"How can you help?"

Jamie transferred himself onto the chaise end of the couch, then shuffled back until he was settled against the seat cushions. "Well, shift up so I can reach," he said with a chuckle. Stephen wriggled a little until his lower legs lay across Jamie's lap. He grabbed Stephen's left leg and proceeded to rub his bare foot, manipulating it, pressing his thumbs into the sole.

"Oh my God, that feels amazing." Stephen's groan had an altogether different sound now. "Don't stop."

"I have to. There's the rest of your leg to see to." He moved to Stephen's calf, taking his time, rubbing and kneading the flesh, then switching to the other leg. "Is that better?"

"Yeah," Stephen said with a sigh. "I did too much, didn't I?"

"Yup."

"Well, you needn't agree so quickly," Stephen groused. "I have aches where I never had aches before." He ran his hands over his inner thighs. "I definitely overdid it on that hip thingy."

Talk about temptation. It was on the tip of Jamie's tongue to ask if he could rub it better, but that was dangerous territory. Especially when Stephen was wearing loose sweats that made it obvious he hadn't bothered to put on any underwear.

Oh my, look at that. Stephen apparently liked being massaged.

Jamie couldn't resist. He slid his hands a little higher over Stephen's knees, and slowly rubbed his lower thighs. Stephen closed his eyes, and his breathing became shallow. Jamie concentrated his efforts on one thigh, kneading it, stroking it, and all the while trying *not* to look at what was going on at Stephen's crotch.

Stephen was evidently big in other areas too.

"That feels good," Stephen murmured. "You have good hands."

What Jamie ached to do with those hands *right this second* would probably have been a step too far.

Probably.

Hey, a guy can dream, right?

"You're amazing too. I watched you. And you did it all with so much ease."

Jamie wasn't about to admit he'd done too

much as well. Stephen would have a field day. "I've been going there a while, remember. But I ached my first time."

Stephen lifted his head from the seat cushion and smirked. "Yeah. Having a nine incher up my butt would make *me* ache too."

He laughed. "Oh, you're definitely getting faster off the mark. My training is obviously working." He stilled his hands on Stephen's thighs. "Maybe a soak in the tub might help," he suggested. "My chair lifts right out." Then he grinned. "Of course, you'd have to fold yourself in two to get in it."

"You're finding this way too amusing."

"I could always give you a full body massage," he said as nonchalantly as he could. He held up his hands. "They're pretty dexterous. As I think I've proved already."

Stephen bit his lip. "You know what? I'll pass. I need to get the dinner sorted anyway." His stomach chose that moment to growl, and he gave Jamie a sheepish glance. "ASAP." He extricated his lower legs from Jamie's grasp and got to his feet. "I'm thinking something quick and simple."

"There's a container of leftover mac and cheese your mom gave us from lunch the other week. It's in the freezer."

"Perfect." Stephen left him and went into the kitchen.

Jamie sagged against the cushions. The way Stephen had sighed as Jamie massaged his calves and feet... The sight of his sweats, tenting...

Shame flooded through him. *I was lusting after him this evening, pure and simple.* Except there had been nothing *remotely* pure about his thoughts. *I'm an awful person.* There still remained that seed of doubt, however, that Stephen had been putting on a show for him. Take the V-Squat as a for instance. It could be done facing either way, but Stephen had chosen to do it with his back to Jamie.

Did he do it on purpose?

Then Jamie gave himself a mental shake. If it was all some attempt at being flirtatious, then why not pursue it when they arrived home? God knew they'd had the opportunity. But there'd been no sign of anything like that. So maybe he *had* imagined it after all.

Damn.

Chapter Fifteen

Baking a cake was turning out to be a lot more entertaining than Jamie had anticipated.

"Hey, this isn't easy!" Stephen paused in the middle of creaming the butter and sugar. "How the hell are you supposed to get this to be fluffy? It's like stirring cement. We should've used a food mixer."

"Agreed, except I can see a teensy little problem with that idea." Jamie gave him a sweet smile. "I don't *possess* a food mixer. Now keep stirring."

Stephen glared at him. "Okay then, Mr. Muscles—*you* do it."

"Hand it over, you wimp."

He picked up the bowl and dumped it in Jamie's lap. "There. *Now* you'll see. Not so easy, is it?"

Jamie beat the solid mass of butter and sugar, and little by little it paled, achieving a fluffy consistency. "Yeah, you were right. Not easy at all. Impossible, even."

"Smartass." Stephen snatched the bowl from his lap, placed it on the countertop, and poured the beaten egg into it. He then began to beat it, the mixture slopping around.

"Hey, aren't you supposed to add it a little at a—"

Stephen glared. "My cake, remember? Anyone can follow a recipe, right? Well, it says to beat in the egg, and that's what I'm doing." He glanced into the bowl, and stilled. "Er… that doesn't look right."

"And how would *you* know? You've never baked before, remember?"

"Okay, so I haven't, but…" He thrust the bowl at Jamie. "*You* look at it, then, and tell me if that looks okay to you."

Jamie peered into the bowl and immediately reached for his phone.

"You're gonna do that *now*?" Stephen wailed. "What on earth are you doing?"

Jamie showed him the screen. "Cake failures and how to fix 'em." He glanced at the site. "Okay, add the flour, quickly, but don't beat it in. You gotta fold it in."

"And what the fuck does that mean?"

Jamie tried to recall watching his mom at work in the kitchen. "Add the flour, but stir the mixture with a sort of figure eight motion." He held out his hand. "Here, I'll show you." He took the bowl and did his best to replicate what he'd seen his mom do. "Like this." He kept the motion slow and steady. "And it looked funny because it was curdling." At least he *thought* that was the word Mom had used, when she was showing Liz how to bake a cake. He could still see Liz standing on a chair at the kitchen table, her face and hands covered in cake mixture. *She must have been about seven years old.*

Stephen folded his arms, covering himself with flour in the process. "Oh really. Well, aren't we the expert? I can see it now. You'll be wanting to take part in the next series of The Great British Baking Show."

Jamie laughed. "Now *there's* a goal." He

glanced into the bowl and smiled. "*That's* better. What's next?"

Stephen grabbed the bowl. "Next is *you* make us some coffee while *I* finish this off and pour it into the baking tin. Then we drink our coffee and wait." He beamed. "This wasn't so bad."

Jamie had a feeling it wasn't over yet.

Stephen stared at the cake pan in dismay. "What happened?" He didn't need to look at Jamie to know he was on his phone. "Tell me we can fix this." The cake was cooked, but it had sunk in the middle. "I can't give this to my mom." It certainly looked nothing like the picture on the recipe.

Jamie sighed. "Well, we can't stick it back in the oven with the hope it'll rise some more, because the rest of it looks done. According to this, there are a couple of explanations. We need to check the oven temperature next time, and maybe cook it in two separate pans, then sandwich them together. And…" He fell silent.

Stephen glanced across at him. "And?"

Jamie bit his lip. "It says don't open the oven door while it's cooking, especially at the beginning."

Well, fuck. "Ah." He narrowed his gaze. "Do *not* say 'I told you so'."

Jamie gave him a wide-eyed stare. "I was going to suggest we cover the top with frosting to disguise it." His lips twitched. "*Then* I was going to say, 'I told you so.'

"I wanted to see how it was doing!" Stephen exclaimed.

"Well, you'll know better next time, won't you?" Jamie retorted.

"And what's this crap about using two cake pans? You never mentioned this when you sent me out to buy one."

"I didn't know, okay? Like I've ever baked before."

They stared at each other for a moment, and then laughter got the better of them. Stephen shook his head. "For a second there, I was going to wrestle you to the ground like I did when we were kids."

Jamie snorted. "Yeah, that was your usual way of trying to win an argument."

"*Trying* to win?" Stephen glared at him. "Name *one* argument I didn't win."

Jamie grinned. "Which was better—a Slurpee or a McFlurry?"

Stephen gaped. "And I was right. A Slurpee is *way* more refreshing."

"Who wants refreshing when there's ice cream to be had?"

"But now you can get Slurpees with vodka or tequila in them."

Jamie snorted. "But I don't *like* vodka or tequila." He laughed. "And here we go again. How about we forget Slurpees and McFlurries, and decide on the frosting we're gonna buy to cover up our disaster of a cake."

They looked at each other for a moment, and then both said simultaneously, "Chocolate."

Stephen smiled. "At least we agree on something." He glanced down at his clothing. "I'll get changed, then I'll go buy some chocolate frosting."

"Yeah, that might be a good idea." Jamie looked like he was dying to laugh.

"What's so funny? Apart from the way the cake looks, of course."

"Turn around." Stephen did as he was told, and Jamie chuckled. "You have these two white handprints on your butt."

Stephen contorted himself trying to see. "How'd they get there?"

"Well, don't look at *me*. I'm sure I'd remember having my hands on your ass." He smirked. "Not a thing I'd be likely to forget."

Stephen stared at him in confusion, then waved his hand. "I'm getting changed." He hurried out of the kitchen and into his bedroom. It was only as he closed the door behind him that the meaning behind Jamie's words truly sank in.

It sounded like Jamie wanted to touch his ass. Maybe as much as Stephen wanted to touch him.

Except that couldn't be right.

Could it?

Mom prized open the cake box, and smiled when she saw the contents. "Oh, look what you bought me. Thank you."

"Correction." Jamie's eyes sparkled. "Look what we *made* you."

Stephen arched his eyebrows. "We?"

"Hey, I helped. I save—" Jamie clammed up.

Mom regarded him with interest. "What were you about to say?"

Stephen gave him a warning glare.

"Oh, nothing. I hope you like chocolate frosting," Jamie said with a smile.

"I love chocolate frosting. Stephen's dad says he wouldn't be surprised to find me eating a bowl of it on its own."

"Oh, that's good, because there's plenty of it on the cake." Jamie's gaze flickered toward Stephen. "In some places more than others."

I am so *going to kick his butt when we get home.* Figuratively speaking.

"Then why don't we cut it up and have some with coffee?" Mom suggested. "You *are* going to stay for cake, aren't you?"

Stephen gave her a wide smile. "Of course we are. It's your birthday."

Dad wandered into the kitchen at that point. "Hey, that looks good. I'm always ready for a slice of cake."

It was Mom's turn to arch her eyebrows. "Imagine that."

Stephen did his best not to laugh.

"I really am impressed, Stephen. I had no idea you could bake." Mom carefully lifted out the cake, using the baking paper Jamie had thoughtfully placed under it. "That was smart," she murmured as she set the cake down on a plate.

Jamie opened his mouth, and Stephen fired him another glance. Jamie promptly mimed zipping his lips. Mom brought a knife to the frosted surface, and Stephen held his breath. She sliced into it and removed the first piece.

"Aha." Mom looked at Stephen over the rim of her glasses, clearly biting back her smile, and he coughed.

"We had a bit of difficulty," he began.

"We?" Jamie stared at him.

Mom burst into laughter. "Oh my, you two. This takes me back, the pair of you sparring with each other." She smiled. "And I'm sure it will taste delicious. There are side plates on the dresser in the dining room, if you want to go get them." Jamie turned his chair in a circle to head that way, but Mom stopped him. "Oh, I didn't mean you of course, sweetheart. Stephen can get them."

Jamie frowned. "I do know where the dining room is. And the dresser. We ate in there, remember?"

"Yes, but Stephen can do it."

Stephen squeezed Jamie's shoulder as he walked past. He hated that his parents couldn't see how their attitude might hurt Jamie. *How can they not see how capable he is?* Then he reflected on his own preconceptions that first day at the pond. His surprise that Jamie could drive. His assumption that Jamie didn't live alone, that he'd need someone around to help him.

I was as bad as Mom. I underestimated him.

Stephen was fairly certain Jamie could do anything he set his mind to. Well, except for some activities that weren't physically possible anymore, unfortunately. Not that Jamie would be interested in them.

Then he reconsidered. *For someone who's not into sex, how come he was paying such attention to my ass?*

"Do you still draw and paint, Jamie?" Stephen's dad asked, getting a stern glare from his wife for speaking with his mouth full.

"Yes, sir. I like to go places and sketch on the weekends." Jamie glanced at Stephen. "Which is how we met up."

"I used to think you'd become a famous painter when you were a boy," his mom said, wiping the corners of her mouth with a napkin. "Now, *Stephen*, bless him…"

Stephen laughed. "I don't think there's an artistic bone in my body."

"Of course not," Jamie murmured. "Whoever heard of an artistic accountant? That's like having a—"

"Yeah, I'm pretty sure you could come up with another combination that's equally unheard of, but don't, okay?" Stephen said quickly.

"Did you take art classes?" his dad asked.

"No, sir. I guess art comes naturally. I did once go to life drawing class though. That was a lot of fun." He placed his fork on his empty plate. "You know, you did all right. It tasted better than it looked."

Stephen rolled his eyes. "Thanks."

"No, really, it was good." Jamie grinned. "Especially the frosting. If that was your first attempt at making frosting, you did really well."

Judging by Stephen's narrowed gaze, Jamie was in for it when they got home.

"Life drawing?" His mom wrinkled her forehead. "You mean, like still life?"

Jamie grinned. "No, ma'am. Naked people." He loved the way her eyes widened.

"People sit around with no clothes on, and you draw them?"

"Or paint them. Me and a whole room of others." Jamie sighed heavily. "But then they lost their funding, and the classes got cut. Pity." He glanced briefly at Stephen before addressing his parents. "One of these days I'd like to take it up again."

"Who would they find to model for something like that?" his mom muttered.

"There were all kinds of people, and all shapes and sizes too. I remember one guy who wore swimming goggles and fins."

His mom blinked. "Fins? Like the kind you wear to go swimming in the ocean?" When Jamie nodded, she shook her head. "It takes all kinds, I guess."

Jamie wasn't really listening at that point. He was in the throes of a brilliant idea. He gazed at Stephen.

I think it's time to do some sketching.

"What are you up to?" Stephen said suddenly.

"Me?" Jamie opened his eyes wide. "I'm sitting

here, contemplating."

"Yeah. It's *what* you're contemplating that worries me."

Jamie merely grinned. *Don't worry. You'll find out soon enough.* Now all he had to do was get Stephen to agree to it.

Chapter Sixteen

Stephen stared through the window at the rain pouring down. "Well, there goes *that* idea." He didn't mind the rain when it amounted to a shower, but this? Hell, even ducks wouldn't venture out in this.

"What's up?" Jamie asked as he came into the living room.

"When I woke up this morning, I had the bright idea of suggesting we visit Horn Pond today, until I looked out the window. Last time I was there, I didn't get to walk around it."

"And that's my fault, right?" Jamie chuckled. "Okay, then let's do something else."

Stephen snorted. "As long as it's not baking another cake."

"Hey, it was delicious. Your mom loved it."

Stephen gaped at him. "It was a disaster."

"Okay, but it was a *delicious* disaster, Mr. Glass-Half-Empty." Jamie regarded him steadily. "I had an idea too for something I wanted to do today, but it would involve you."

"I know I'm going to regret this, but go on, tell me."

"Can I draw your portrait?"

Stephen stared. "Seriously? Why would you want to do that?"

Jamie rolled his eyes. "Duh. You'd be wonderful to draw. And there's no one else here.

Please?" He batted his lashes.

"Enough with the Bambi eyes." Stephen considered the proposal. "Would I have to make like a statue? Because I don't think I can sit as still as the lion in the park."

Jamie laughed. "You *can* move, doof. Just don't go waving your arms around." His eyes sparkled. "The picture will end up all blurry."

He laughed. "Okay, I'll do it. How do you want me? Will these clothes do?"

Jamie sighed. "I'll be concentrating on your face, so what you're wearing won't matter. Let me go get my sketch pad and pencils." He rolled himself out of the room.

Stephen smiled to himself. He was curious to see how the portrait turned out.

"Oh my dear Lord."

He headed for Jamie's room quickly. "You okay?" he called out.

When he got there, Jamie was staring at his phone and smiling. "Wait till you see what my mom sent me. She found a photo of us. We must have been about nine or ten." He held up the phone for Stephen to see. "Check this out."

Stephen peered at the screen. "Oh my." It had been taken at Halloween, the pair of them posing by the front door of Jamie's house. "I'd forgotten about this." He preened. "I made a great Han Solo, don't you think?" Then he snickered. "And you made a gorgeous Leia." He glanced at Jamie. "You say you were *how* old when you realized you were gay?"

Jamie hit him with the sketch pad. "Hey, I'm gay, not a cross-dresser. And remind me. How come

I ended up as Leia?"

"I was too big for the costume, remember?"
He shook his head. They were happy days.

"Well, come on, I'm ready." Jamie patted the sketch pad. "You can sit on the couch, so at least you'll be comfortable. I'll stay in my chair."

Stephen followed him into the living room, and flopped down onto the couch. He struck a dramatic pose, his legs sticking up into the air. "How's this?"

Jamie laughed. "Awful. Sit up."

He did as instructed. "Seriously though, how do you want me?"

Jamie gazed at him for a moment, then obviously relented. "Okay, you can lie down, with your head on some cushions, face turned toward me. You might as well be comfortable."

Stephen stretched out, and then relaxed his body. "This okay?"

"Perfect." Jamie opened the sketch pad. "Just don't go falling asleep, all right?"

Stephen gaped. "How long is this going to take?"

"Oh, I should be done by dinner time." Jamie's eyes sparkled with humor. "Just relax, okay? You can talk, but don't wriggle."

Stephen sighed. "I don't think I have the patience for this."

Jamie gave him a hard stare. "Any man who can sit through the whole Lord of the Rings trilogy in one day has plenty of patience, trust me."

"Hey, you said I could choose what we watched."

Jamie grinned. "A decision I later regretted.

Now keep still."

Stephen did a Jamie and mimed zipping his lips.

If I end up looking like Pennywise, I am so *going to kill him.*

Stephen stretched, glad of the chance to move. He'd lain on the couch for a couple of hours, and he had to admit, it had been pleasant. They'd chatted about high school for most of the time, for which he was grateful. He'd shared enough of his personal life, and had no desire to talk more on the subject. School was kind of a neutral topic.

"You're obviously used to multitasking," Stephen commented. "Seeing as you can draw *and* talk at the same time."

"Female brain wiring," Jamie murmured, his focus on the paper.

"Excuse me?"

He glanced up. "I read once that women are better at multitasking, because of how their brains are wired. So I guess my brain works more like a woman's." He frowned. "Can't *you* multitask?"

"Hell no." Stephen snorted. "I have to turn off the radio when I'm trying to parallel park."

Jamie chuckled. "Yup. Definitely a male brain." He laid down his pencil. "Wanna see?"

Stephen was off that couch like his ass was on fire. "You bet." He took the pad from Jamie and gazed at it. "Oh…. Oh wow." Jamie had captured his likeness perfectly, except…

"Is that a good 'Oh wow'?"

Stephen stared at the beautiful drawing. "It's… it's me, but it's not me."

Jamie cackled. "Okay, that makes perfect sense."

He struggled to put his feelings into words. "You've brought an added something to it, and I'm not sure what that is." He gazed at it. "Is this really how you see me?"

"You don't like it."

Stephen jerked his head up. "No! That's not it at all." Damn, why was this so difficult? "You made me look better than I am."

Jamie blinked. "But that's how I see you."

He smiled. "Then I wish other men saw me the same way."

Jamie laughed. "You should've seen some of the paintings and sketches at that life class. Some of them… it was hard to believe we were all drawing the same model."

Stephen stared at him. "You really went to those classes? I thought that was something you invented for my mom."

He chuckled. "Sure I went."

"But… wasn't it weird?"

Jamie frowned. "Why would it be weird? None of the models had two dicks or three nipples, or even a second head."

"Yeah, but… seeing people naked…"

Jamie sighed. "The aim of the class was to improve technique. It was kinda… clinical. It's not like I got turned on, staring at a naked guy wearing swimming goggles and fins." Then his eyes widened. "Oh, *I* get it. You'd be nervous doing something like that."

"No, I wouldn't," Stephen retorted.

"Oh yeah? Prove it." Jamie grinned. "I dare ya."

Fuck. He had to say that, didn't he? There was no way Stephen was going to let him win.

He lifted his chin and met Jamie's amused gaze. "How do you want me?" He removed his sweater, then squirmed out of his jeans as fast as he could before he had time to change his mind. When all that remained was his underwear, he paused, standing awkwardly, hands by his sides.

"You're serious." Jamie's eyes were huge. Then he smirked as he glanced at Stephen's briefs. "Apparently not. Still chicken, huh?"

Stephen snorted. "You wish." Then he took a deep breath, grasped the waistband of his briefs, and pushed them down his legs, stepping out of them and tossing them aside as nonchalantly as he could manage. He straightened, and disconcertingly his dick filled a little. Thankfully, Jamie didn't comment.

"Lie back down on the couch," Jamie instructed.

He did as he was told, then followed more instructions to bend one leg, put an arm behind his head, tilt his head so…. The instructions helped calm his nerves and focus him. When Jamie was satisfied, he picked up his pencil and began drawing again.

"You doing okay there?" Jamie asked.

Stephen gave a nervous chuckle. "Well, I definitely didn't see *this* coming."

"There will be no coming, you hear?" Jamie's eyes glittered mischievously. "Because if any of *that* lands on my sketch pad, you'll ruin it."

Stephen caught his breath for a moment, then laughed. "I can't believe you said that."

"But it made you laugh, right? Now lie still."

Stephen breathed deeply, then relaxed his body. It took him a few minutes to realize it was no different to Jamie drawing his face. He recalled Jamie's comment about it being clinical, and that helped. *I never thought I'd be doing this.* But he had to admit, it was sort of liberating. He was lying naked on the couch, the rain hitting the windows, and Jamie's pencil was flying over his sketch pad.

Based on how his portrait had turned out, Stephen couldn't wait to see the next one.

"You're a joy to draw," Jamie murmured, looking up from his pad. He'd already worked on three or four sheets, and had removed them from the pad to work on another.

"I bet you say that to all your models," Stephen teased, but he couldn't deny Jamie's comment made him feel good. He tightened his stomach, liking the way Jamie's breathing hitched the tiniest bit.

"Lift your head a little," Jamie requested. When Stephen did so, he smiled. "That's it. I love the line of your body, the curve of your arm."

"That doesn't sound very clinical," Stephen remarked. Not that he minded.

Jamie's eyes were warm. "Hard to be clinical when I'm looking at you." His lips twitched. "And speaking of hard…"

Stephen didn't need to glance down to know he

had an erection. His cheeks grew hot. "Sorry about that."

"Don't you dare apologize." Jamie's gaze moved lower. "You have a beautiful dick."

"You think?" Stephen longed to know whether it was Jamie the artist talking, or Jamie the gay man.

Jamie nodded. "I love the way it curves up, so thick and long." He locked gazes with Stephen. "You're beautiful, period."

Stephen swallowed, lost for words.

Jamie tilted his head. "Has no one ever told you that?"

"Maybe once or twice, usually the first time we…" He didn't want to think about that. Because when the compliments stopped, other things started.

"If you were *my* man, I'd tell you every day. I'd share how much I loved your broad chest, your arms, the curve of your thighs…" Jamie shook his head, smiling. "And part of you obviously likes that idea."

Stephen had to look. His cock was pointing toward the ceiling. He raised his chin and looked Jamie in the eye. "You don't mind?"

"Why should I mind? You obviously don't. That's how it should be between artist and model."

Stephen took a deep breath. "You don't talk to me like I'm your model."

Jamie smiled. "It's not like it's the first time I've seen you naked."

He blinked. "Huh?"

"Sure. Have you forgotten? Your grandma's place in Florida? We went skinny-dipping in her pool one night, it was so hot. Thankfully no one caught us."

Stephen chuckled. "I think we looked very

different then."

Jamie smirked. "Trust me. You've improved with age. Plus, you've grown. In all directions." Another not-so-subtle glance at his cock.

He smiled, giving the slightest push of his hips in Jamie's direction, his dick pointing directly at him.

Jamie's lips parted. "Yep. Definitely a beautiful cock." Then he laid down his pencil. "I think we're done."

Stephen reached for his jeans and pulled them on, leaving the waistband unbuttoned. "Let me see." He went over to where Jamie had placed the sheets of paper on the coffee table, and as he gazed at them, his throat tightened.

Jamie had done a series of sketches, one of his head and shoulders, another of his torso from neck to his pubes, and yet another of his legs. But the one that caught his eye was a detailed drawing of his dick, capturing every detail, even the vein that ran along its length, the way his pubes curled about its base, the shine on the taut head...

Stephen forced out a chuckle. "Wow. Easy to see which part caught your eye."

Jamie grinned. "Well, what do you expect when you give me material like that to work with?" He collected the sheets together.

"What are you going to do with them?"

Jamie smiled. "I'm going to frame them, and hang them up in the living room." When Stephen gasped, he laughed. "Like shooting fish in a barrel. Don't panic. I'm going to put them on my bedroom wall."

"Why... why would you want to do that?"

Stephen wasn't sure how he felt about Jamie gazing at his naked body day after day.

"So I can look at you," Jamie locked gazes with him.

The look sent a shiver through him.

Jamie darted a glance at his crotch. "Hey, if you wanna walk around the house all day like that, I'm not gonna complain." Stephen peered down to where his jeans were open, revealing the fuzz of his pubes. Hastily he tugged the zipper, and Jamie sighed. "Damn. I should've kept my mouth shut."

Stephen was at a loss to know how to react. Jamie was confusing the hell out of him.

His phone buzzed to announce the arrival of a text, and Stephen grabbed it from the table, grateful for the interruption. He didn't recognize the number or the name.

Hey. My name is Trey. Carl told me to look you up if I was ever in Boston.

Stephen froze. Why the fuck would his ex tell some guy to look him up? Then another text arrived.

He's told me all about you. Can't wait to hook up to find out if it's all true…

That was all the impetus Stephen needed to switch off his phone and toss it onto the couch, as though its touch burned his fingers.

"Are you okay?" Jamie's voice was laced with concern.

"I'm fine." Stephen pasted on a smile that he didn't feel in the slightest. "Can modeling wear you out? Because I think lying still for so long has made me feel tired." It was the only excuse he could think of to leave the room.

"Maybe you need a nap," Jamie suggested.

He nodded eagerly. "I think you're right. I'll go put my head down for an hour. That might help." And with that, he left the living room, walked into his bedroom, and closed the door behind him. He lay on his bed and stared at the ceiling, his hands laced behind his head.

Stephen could only guess at what Carl had told his buddy Trey, but he was willing to bet Trey was out of the same mold as that fucker. Not that Stephen had any intention of hooking up with him.

Is it something about me that draws these guys? Some flaw that only abusive assholes could sense, and it pulled them to him, like moths to a flame. Some weakness that made them want to move in and exploit it.

He pushed such thoughts aside. They only served to make him feel bad. What sent guilt flooding through him was what had just happened.

How could I act like that? He knew he was flirting, but that was because Jamie was flirting too. *Flirting? That was* way *more than flirting.* Jamie's remarks left him hot and flustered, and Stephen was still confused by them. *Why would he flirt with me? It's not like we're going to* do *anything, right?* Which made Stephen's responses even worse. It felt too much like he was leading Jamie on. Because Jamie wouldn't want a guy like Stephen.

Why would he? Suppose by some miracle we could make it work… Why would he want that? And even if he did, who's to say I wouldn't go and ruin it?

Because his past was a pattern of relationship fails.

The blame for *some* of those failures surely had to lie on him.

Chapter Seventeen

Jamie scribbled notes on a pad beside his bowl of cereal, now and again pausing to eat and drink his coffee. Monday mornings were when he planned out his week. He could hear Stephen bustling around, and he frowned. The way he'd left the room in such a hurry the previous afternoon... And he'd been quiet most of the evening too.

Did I push him too far yesterday? Jamie hadn't thought so at the time. In fact, Stephen had appeared to be relaxed once he'd gotten over his initial nerves. Jamie still couldn't believe he'd agreed to it. But what a gorgeous model...

Jamie had gone to bed that night and had lain there gazing at the sketches while he tugged on his dick. He knew his subsequent boner had nothing to do with what was going on inside his head and everything to do with his hand, but it still felt good.

A guy can dream, right? And he *had* dreamed that night, of falling asleep in Stephen's arms, of sharing kiss after kiss, of Stephen's hands caressing him, making him hard.

Was I too subtle? If *Jamie* had been on the receiving end of such obvious flirting, he'd have had no doubt as to the speaker's intentions. But Stephen hadn't taken him up on it.

"Good morning." Stephen came into the kitchen, dressed in his suit. Jamie loved seeing him in it.

Let's face it. He'd make a burlap sack look good.

"Ready for a new week? Raring to go?" Jamie teased. Stephen was *not* a morning person.

Stephen merely gave him a look, then proceeded to smother a bagel with cream cheese.

"I've been thinking," Jamie began, peering at his notes. "I might take a short vacation soon. There's a natural gap coming up in my schedule, and I can't remember the last time I went on vacation."

Stephen nodded. "Sounds like a good idea."

Jamie waited, but when nothing else was forthcoming, he held out his mug. "Can I have a refill while you're over there?" Anything to get Stephen talking.

"Sure." Stephen took it and poured coffee.

What Jamie *longed* to do was ask Stephen to come with him. Sure, he had work, but he could take time off, right?

"I mean, I know I've talked about skiing, but that's not till after New Year's." He gazed at Stephen. "When did you last take a vacation?"

Stephen smiled. "I lived in San Diego, remember? The beach was right on my doorstep. I could go surfing and swimming every weekend."

"Ah, but did you?"

Stephen sighed. "Yeah. I used to love going to visit Marie and the kids. We'd spend whole days on the beach."

That did it. Jamie was going to ask him along. He'd worked damn hard since the move back to Boston. *His dad wouldn't begrudge him a week off, surely?* Besides, the thought of spending a relaxing vacation somewhere warm was pushing Jamie's buttons. *Someplace warm enough that I can get him into some teeny tiny shorts.*

Yum.

"I've been thinking too," Stephen said suddenly as he walked over to the table, carrying two mugs. He went back for his bagel and joined Jamie. "Maybe I *should* start looking for a place of my own."

Jamie stilled. "Oh?" His heart sank. He'd gotten the impression Stephen was going to share with him a while longer. Hardly any time had passed since he'd moved in.

"Yeah. Well, I can't live here forever, can I?" Stephen gave a half smile that didn't reach his eyes.

Why not? The words were right there on the tip of Jamie's tongue. "When were you thinking of starting your search?"

"No time like the present," Stephen said brightly. "I was going to take a look online during my lunch break today, and make some appointments to view for this week. Maybe after work."

Shit, he was really serious about this.

"Mind if I tag along?" Jamie asked, his tone even.

Stephen blinked. "Actually, I *was* going to ask you if you wanted to. I'd value your opinion. Besides, if my best friend hates it, he's hardly likely to come visit, right?"

"Then I *will* be getting an invite?" That was something, at least.

"Of course!" Stephen's smile was more genuine. "I'll get started today." And with that, he took a big bite out of his bagel, and peered at his phone.

Should I be grateful he's keeping me in his life? Jamie knew one thing. He did *not* want Stephen to go. *What the hell am I doing wrong?* His usual positivity deserted him for a moment, and he wracked his brains for some clue as to what he'd done to bring about such a drastic decision.

The only thing he could point to was the nude drawing. He'd made it obvious he was interested, and Stephen was running. Maybe Jamie wasn't seeing the situation correctly, but right then he was a mess. What he needed was some good advice.

And he knew exactly who to ask.

"Want to tell me why I'm here? And during my lunch break?" Liz grinned. "Not that I would *ever* say no to bubble tea and a coconut fro-yo."

Jamie's salted caramel frozen yogurt was delicious, but he'd hardly touched it. He put down his spoon and clasped his hands together on the table. "Am I ugly?"

Liz blinked. "Excuse me?"

"Serious question. Am I ugly? It's okay. You can say it if I am. I'm not some little snowflake. I can take criticism." He stuck out his chin.

Liz bit her lip. "Bro, you're cute. You're a good-looking guy." She cocked her head. "Does that make you feel better?"

He ignored the question. "Am I boring, then?"

Liz put down her spoon and rested her chin on her laced fingers. "Okay, what's going on?"

He sighed. "I'm trying to come up with reasons why Stephen wouldn't want to date me."

She gazed at him thoughtfully. "Well… does he know you're interested?" She reached for her tea.

Jamie gaped. "Oh, I *get* it now. I'm being too subtle. I need a sign that says, Take Me I'm Yours." He shrugged. "I thought drawing a detailed portrait of his dick was enough of a hint, but go figure."

Liz spluttered tea all over the tabletop. Jamie handed her napkins, and she hastily wiped up her mess. When she was done, she gave him a frank stare. "You drew him naked?" Jamie nodded, and her lips twitched. "What does his dick look like?"

Jamie gaped in mock horror. "You shouldn't be asking questions like that."

"Why not? I want to know." She leaned in closer. "Well? Is he… big?"

Jamie mimicked her body language. "Looking at it made my mouth water."

Liz erupted into a loud coughing fit. "Okay," she said, wiping her lips. "That was more information than I needed." She leaned back and scowled at him. "Shame on you."

"For what?" Jamie stared at her, perplexed.

"For assuming there's one damn thing wrong with you. If Stephen doesn't want to date you, it's because of something *he's* hung up on, not something about you. Because any man alive would be damn lucky to be dating you."

"Any man alive, huh?" Jamie smirked. "Maybe

that's where I'm going wrong. I need to start looking at dead guys."

"I'm being serious!" Liz's eyes flashed. "And my advice is, talk to Stephen. I still think you're perfect for each other. I also think he needs glasses if he can't see what's right under his nose." She shook her head. "I can't believe you got him to model for you. Boy, you must have some special set of skills."
He preened, and she laughed. "Now go use them again on Stephen."

He sighed. "I'm meeting him at a house after he finishes work."

"What house?"

"Oh, just some house he's thinking of buying," he said lightly, though his heart was heavy at the thought. "I'm going along to give him my opinion."

Liz pressed her lips together.

"What are you thinking?"

She frowned. "I'm thinking I'd like to give him *my* opinion. I'd tell him to stay where he is and date my brother."

Jamie reached across the table and squeezed her hand. "I'm glad I've got you in my corner."

"Always."

He relinquished her hand. "Now finish your tea and fro-yo. Your break is almost over."

As Liz collected her purse and coat from the back of her chair, she gave him a reassuring glance. "He's not going to be like all the others. I can feel it."

Jamie hoped not. He wasn't sure if he could take that, not from Stephen.

The realtor gave Stephen a broad smile. "I'll be out in my car when you're done. You know, to give you both time to discuss the property." Her gaze flickered in Jamie's direction, taking in both him and the chair, and then she left them in the middle of a large empty living room.

At least she'd addressed him. Some people acted like he was invisible.

Jamie bit his lip. "Are you thinking what *I'm* thinking?"

Stephen frowned. "What?"

"It was that last bit about giving us *both* time." Jamie grinned. "She thinks we're a couple. We're obviously house-hunting for our future love nest."

Stephen jerked his head toward the door she'd used. "Seriously?"

He didn't appear to find the concept amusing, so Jamie quickly changed the subject. "Okay, what do you think? Personally, I like the neighborhood. It's got lots of trees, quiet streets, and I haven't heard a single gunshot since we got here. Unless she's bribed all the drug dealers to keep it down till we leave. That's a definite possibility."

Stephen rolled his eyes. "God, you come out with some shit, feather-brain."

He beamed. "That's my job, right? But seriously… what do you think of the place?" He could picture Stephen living there. The back yard was on the small side, but he imagined Stephen would hire someone to take care of it, while he made sure there was enough space for a grill and a lounger.

Stephen sighed. "Nope. It won't do."

"Why? What's wrong with it?" Nothing that Jamie could see, unless Stephen already had a definite picture of what he wanted.

"Well, you only have to think about it for a second to realize it won't do. I had to get you up three steps, for one thing. The doorways aren't wide enough because this isn't a modern house. So we're talking widening doorways, putting in a ramp… and that's just for starters."

"Wait a second." Jamie took a breath. "*You're* the one who'll be living here, right?"

"Yes, but *you'll* be visiting, won't you? I'm not buying a place that isn't wheelchair accessible, and that's that."

That was it. Jamie was confused as fuck.

Stephen wanted a place that Jamie would be able to access, so presumably that meant he wanted Jamie to stick around. *All well and good.*

But it *wasn't* good.

I'm okay to be his best friend, but not his boyfriend?

Why the fuck didn't Stephen want Jamie the way Jamie wanted Stephen?

Then he reconsidered. *What am I expecting Stephen to do, read my mind?* It wasn't as if Stephen had asked him out and Jamie had turned him down. And for someone who claimed to be a positive person, Jamie was drawing some very glass-half-empty conclusions.

Hey, even positive people can suffer from a lack

of confidence occasionally.

There *was* one explanation of course, for the lack of any move on Stephen's part, but Jamie did *not* want to go there. Because to do that would mean Liz was wrong, *he* was wrong, and Stephen was no different from every other guy he'd wanted to date.

Except Stephen was already *nothing like* those guys. For one thing, Jamie hadn't been in love with them.

"I'm ready to leave," Stephen announced, and headed for the door. Jamie followed, the wheels of the chair finding little purchase against the carpet.
Once outside, Stephen spoke quietly with the realtor, they shook hands, and she drove away. "Meet you back home?" he said, pointing his key at his car.

Jamie nodded. Not that it would be Stephen's home for much longer.

"You've been quiet all night," Stephen commented as he channel-hopped. There was nothing grabbing his attention on TV, and Jamie seemed lost in his own little world. That was *so* not like him that the hairs lifted on the back of Stephen's neck, and something quivered in his stomach.

"Yeah. Stuff on my mind." Jamie sat on the chaise end, his legs stretched out in front of him. A TV guide lay on his lap, but he wasn't really looking at it.

"Want to share? You know what they say about

a problem…"

Jamie closed the guide and stared at him. "Maybe you could help at that."

"Anything," Stephen declared. Anything was better than the uncomfortable silence that had lain between them.

Jamie turned his head to look Stephen in the eye. "Do you think I'm attractive?"

Chapter Eighteen

Stephen blinked. "Excuse me?" He aimed the remote at the TV and switched it off.

"It's a simple enough question. Do you find me attractive?" Jamie repeated.

"Okay, I'll play along. Yes." Stephen's heartbeat was climbing, however.

"How attractive?" Jamie demanded. "Say, on a scale where #1 is the Elephant Man, and #10 is Chris Evans."

Talk about being put on the spot. "No fair."

"Why not?""

"Because… well… I'd have to give you an #11." Jamie's eyes lit up, and Stephen knew he'd given the right answer. Except now he had questions of his own. "Now tell me why you're fishing for compliments."

Jamie studied him for a moment, and Stephen's skin erupted in goose bumps.

"Because I don't have a clue how you see me," Jamie said simply.

Stephen went with humor. "Duh."

Jamie clearly wasn't having it. "I'm being serious here. Do you see me as Jamie the BFF? Jamie the roommate? Or… in some whole other way?"

Okay, *that* got his attention.

"What other way were you thinking of?" Stephen asked in a low voice.

"Oh, I don't know." Jamie's tone was light and breezy, and nothing like the careful way he'd framed that last question. "I sorta like the sound of Jamie the… boyfriend."

Stephen stared at him in silence. Except the blood pounding in his ears wasn't quiet, and neither was his heartbeat. *How in the hell do I answer that?*

Jamie gave a single nod. "I guess that's a no then."

"No!" he blurted out. "I mean, it's not a no. I mean… you want to date *me*?"

Jamie laughed out loud. "Of *course* I wanna date you. On the aforementioned scale, you're at least a 12. You're gorgeous. Considerate. Plus, you have so many good qualities. You don't leave crumbs in my bed, you don't clip your toenails in there either…." His breathing hitched. "And that's kinda where I'd like you right now."

"In your bed?" Not that the idea hadn't crossed his mind about a million times. Jamie nodded, his gaze locked on Stephen's. "Oh. I see."

"Well, *you* might, but *I* don't," Jamie murmured. "Because if I'm an 11, why aren't you jumping up and down at the idea of sleeping with me?" His eyes twinkled. "Not that we'd get much sleeping done."

Stephen's heart pounded. "Can I be honest?" Because right then he saw no other way forward but to tell the truth.

"Uh-oh. Not sure I like the sound of that." Jamie's expression grew a little more guarded.

"I think you're gorgeous—"

"Okay, this is going better than I thought,"

Jamie interjected.

"But—"

"Aw crap, there's a but."

"Jamie! For God's sake, let me finish a fucking *sentence*, okay?"

He stilled, his eyes wide.

Stephen didn't want to do this. He didn't want to be yet another guy who let Jamie down, but he didn't see a way through this. "I didn't make a move on you because…. Jesus, how do I put this?"

"Just say it," Jamie gritted out. "Because this is killing me."

"You don't want to be with someone like me," he said at last.

Jamie stared at him. "Why would I not want to be with a gorgeous, caring, generous, sweet man?"

"Because I'm a loser."

Jamie gaped at him, his lips parted but no sound coming from them.

"You ever stop to think why all those guys were with me? That maybe it was my fault? That something in me *attracted* them? I went into every relationship expecting the worst, and that is exactly what I got. I let them walk all over me, because I thought if I did whatever they wanted, they'd change. And of course they didn't."

"But this is bullshit," Jamie said bluntly. "I am *nothing like* those guys. Yes, there's something about you that attracts me to you, and you wanna know what it is? Your sweet nature. That hasn't changed, because you were a sweet kid back then. Your kindness. Your honesty. Your… goodness, if you like."

"Don't," Stephen urged him. "Don't do this.

Don't put me up on some pedestal, because I will sure as shit fall from it, and when I do, I'll hurt you in the process."

Jamie's eyes widened. "What is it you're not telling me?"

Damn his intuition.

There was nowhere else to go but with the whole truth.

"Jamie… I'm not into platonic relationships, okay? If I'm with a guy, I like to be… *with* a guy, if you get my drift."

Jamie became so still. "Let's pretend for the moment that I don't. Spell it out."

Stephen couldn't look at him. "The one factor all my past relationships had in common? Was the sex. I like sex, pure and simple. And I like a lot of it. Which is why all those guys liked dating me. At the start, it was all about the fucking." That came out blunter than he'd intended, but maybe that was how it had to be to drive the message home.

Then he recalled the text from Carl's buddy, Trey. "I know I don't talk about my past relationships, but this might give you a clue. The other day I got a text from some guy who said my ex had given him my number. He wanted to hook up. I don't know what Carl told him, but I'll make a guess. Carl probably told him I'd be a good fuck, and that if Trey wanted to get real rough, I'd be okay with it." His heart hammered. "After all, I took everything Carl dished out, right?" Until he'd found the strength to walk away.

"Is that why you got a new phone? Mom asked why you hadn't kept your old number."

"You're damn straight I got a new phone. I don't want any contact with anyone from my past."

Jamie fell silent for a moment, as though mentally digesting his words. Then he gave Stephen a frank stare. "Why would *anything* you've said prevent us from being together?"

He swallowed. "I know if we were a couple, that part of our life would have to take a back seat. I'm just glad you got to have sex before the accident."

Jamie frowned. "What do you mean?"

"Well, I don't know about you, but the thought of being a virgin my whole life…"

Jamie *stared* at him.

"What? I mean, it's not like you can…"

That stare didn't waver.

"I mean, can you even…? Do you get…?"

Jamie swallowed. "And you can stop right there."

"Jamie?" Jesus, his face was so *hard*.

"Do you think about sex?"

Stephen frowned. "I think you already know the answer to that one."

"Do you get turned on by what you see, what you read?"

"Well… yeah."

Jamie nodded slowly. "Well, here's a fucking newsflash for ya. So do I. Yes, I *can* have sex. Yes, I *do* get boners. Guess what? I jerk off too. Granted, my orgasms are probably not what *you'd* expect, but yeah, I have them." He reached for his chair, and transferred into it.

"Jamie…" Stephen had well and truly fucked it up this time.

Jamie ignored him, and wheeled himself down the hall to his room.

Do *something, you idiot.*

Stephen lurched up off the couch and followed him. "Jamie, I'm—"

Jamie turned his chair around and faced him. "And now, if you don't mind, you can leave me alone to play with my toys. Yes, I'm talking sex toys, because here's another exclusive for you—people with disabilities use toys too. So I'll be considerate and not moan *too* loud when I'm jacking off. I wouldn't want to disturb you. Now get the fuck out of my room." His eyes were like flint.

Stephen knew they were done. "Okay," he said softly. He left the room, wincing at the sound of it slamming shut behind him.

"You know what *really* fucking hurts about all this?" The pain in Jamie's voice lanced right through him. "I thought you'd be different. I thought you wouldn't make assumptions. Christ, all you had to do to make it freaking perfect was kiss me and ask me what I like to do in bed, and I'd have been yours, heart, body and soul. And no, I *don't* have much experience, but you do. I was kinda hoping you'd share it."

"I fucked up, all right?" Stephen yelled. "But that doesn't mean I can't make things right. At least let me try."

The silence that fell so heavily didn't bode well.

"Please, Jamie. I'm not asking you to let me in there. Not now. But I *am* asking you to give me another chance."

Silence.

Come on, Jamie. You know *you want this.* Because *he* sure did.

"Go to sleep, Stephen. You've got work tomorrow." Jamie's voice had lost its harsh edge, and he sounded bone tired.

"Say you'll give me another chance. I promise I won't let you down." This was too fucking important.

Jamie's heartfelt sigh reached his ears. "I need to sleep."

"I know. And I am *so* fucking sorry I hurt you. You're right. I shouldn't have made assumptions." His heart felt as if it were about to break.

"Damn straight."

Stephen strove to find the words that would fix this. "This is all new to me, but I want to learn. Yes, I'm nervous. I don't want to screw this up any more than I already have. But at least say we can talk about this, and *not* through a closed door."

The quiet was torture.

"Tomorrow." Jamie spoke so softly that Stephen had to strain to hear him. "We'll talk tomorrow night when you get home, okay?"

"Okay." Relief flooded through him.

"Goodnight."

Stephen leaned forward, his forehead touching the door. "Goodnight, Jamie." Then he walked slowly into the living room to retrieve his phone, his heart aching.

Looks like I've got some research to do. Because he wasn't going to sleep until he had answers to his questions.

I'm going to put this right. If Jamie would let

him.

Jamie wasn't ready to sleep, although the confrontation had exhausted him. Heaviness pervaded his chest and arms, and he felt cold, right to the core. His mind scrambled to take it all in.

He needed comfort, solace, hope.

He needed his mom.

Jamie composed a short text, hoping she hadn't already gone to bed. When his phone buzzed and he saw the screen, the tightness in his chest eased.

What's up, baby boy?

She'd called him that so many times, and right then he yearned to hear her voice. *Can we talk?*

Seconds later the phone warbled. "Hey. What's wrong? And don't tell me there's nothing wrong. Call it a mother's instincts."

He poured it all out, holding nothing back. She'd seen him at his worst, at his lowest, and he knew with all his heart that she wouldn't offer platitudes but good, solid advice.

"So are you going to give him a second chance?" she asked when he was done.

The wounded part of his soul wanted to say no, but Jamie knew as soon as he'd finished talking to Stephen through his bedroom door that he would. "Yeah."

"I'm glad. I'd hate to see your friendship end like this."

"End?" Then it hit him. She was right. If they couldn't find a way back from this, continuing forward would be painful.

"You love him, don't you?"

Jamie sighed. "Mom, I loved him like a brother. Then he came back, all grown up and gorgeous, and I loved him even more. And part of me hoped he could love me too."

"That's because you always see the best in people. You didn't think he'd be like all the rest."

"Now and again, the thought did creep into my mind, but I pushed it away. And I *kept on* pushing it away, right up to the moment when he made it obvious how he sees me."

"Has he told you he loves you?"

"No. Not that I gave him a chance to get that far."

"Then that's why you need to talk. Find out how he really feels about you. Have faith, baby boy. Believe in him."

"After everything he said?"

There was a pause. "Right now you're hurting. I understand that. But what you need to do is sleep. It's a great healer, and you need to be ready to listen to him tomorrow with an open mind and an open heart. Tomorrow is anothah day after all, Scarlett."

He laughed softly. "You'd have been perfect as Melanie Hamilton."

"And as for Stephen… It sounds to me like he's trying to make amends, so let him. Hear him out. Who knows where such a conversation might lead?"

"Love you," he said suddenly.

"Love you too. Now get some sleep, and call me

when you've talked with Stephen. You two are going to be in my thoughts."

"Thanks, Mom." He said goodnight and disconnected the call. After placing his phone on the nightstand, he lay back and stared at the ceiling.

Tomorrow is another day.

Mom was right. Who knew what the situation would be come tomorrow night? He switched off the lamp, closed his eyes, and waited for sleep to take away the ache in his heart.

Chapter Nineteen

Jamie pushed down on the arms of his wheelchair, lifting himself up a little and holding still for about thirty seconds. *Gotta give that butt some respite, right?* Then he settled back into the chair and stared at the monitor, trying not to think about Stephen.

Not that he'd seen Stephen that morning. By the time Jamie emerged from his room, bleary-eyed and still tired, Stephen had already left for work. Jamie took one look at the empty kitchen, poured himself a coffee, then went back to bed to catch another hour of sleep.

By the time lunch had come and gone, he was feeling considerably more alert. Now and again he glanced at his phone, wondering if Stephen would message him.

Nothing.

In the end, he put the phone out of sight and threw himself into his work. Easier said than done, however. His mind kept replaying the previous evening's conversation, until he couldn't think straight. He told himself things would improve when Stephen got home.

If Jamie hadn't gone mad by then.

At four-thirty, the front door opened.

"Stephen? That you?"

Stephen poked his head around the living room door. "Unless you gave some burglars a key, yes."

God, he looked like Jamie felt. There were dark smudges under his eyes, and a tightness in his face. A tiny part of Jamie was happy he wasn't the only one suffering. Then Jamie pushed that thought right out of his head. Such meanness was out of line.

"What are you doing home at this hour?"

Stephen came into the room and removed his jacket, after placing his bag on the couch. "I asked if I could leave early. Under the circumstances, Dad said yes."

"What circumstances?"

"Seeing as he'd gotten so little work out of me today, he figured I might as well go home." Stephen gave him a wry smile. "Hey, he's not about to fire me, right? And I'll work overtime to make up for it." He walked over to Jamie's desk and stood beside it. "I'm sorry," he said quietly. "You were right last night. I shouldn't have made assumptions. That was idiotic."

Jamie folded his arms. "If you're looking for disagreement from me, you're not gonna find it."

"I don't expect to." Stephen expelled a breath. "I did a lot of thinking about what you said. Did some reading too." His lips twitched. "In fact, I was reading today when I should have been working."

"That might account for your lack of productivity." Jamie tilted his head to one side. "What were you reading?"

Stephen went over to the couch and reached into his bag. He removed a Kindle, opened the cover and dragged his finger across the screen. Then he handed it to Jamie. "This."

Jamie stared at the book cover. "When did you buy this?"

"My Kindle? I've had that a while."

Jamie rolled his eyes. "You know what I mean. When did you buy this book?" It had a cartoon cover, but what caught Jamie's attention instantly was the title: *A Quick & Easy Guide To Sex & Disability.*

Something fluttered in Jamie's belly, and his heart felt a little lighter.

"Last night. About twenty minutes after we spoke through your door. It's not a huge read, but I've already gone through it three or four times."

"Did you make notes?" Jamie joked.

To his surprise, Stephen nodded. "Then I found a few websites that gave me even more to think about."

Jamie was speechless.

"So, I guess I'm asking… can we start again, please? Because I've got an idea how we might do that."

Jamie cleared his throat. "What did you have in mind?"

"You got anything planned for dinner?"

Jamie chuckled. "Er, no, doof, because it's *your* turn to cook, remember?"

Stephen smiled. "Perfect. In that case, grab a shower and put on your Sunday best, because we're eating out."

"Sunday best?" Jamie snorted. "I'm assuming that means we're not eating at a fast food joint."

"Absolutely not. I'm taking you to dinner someplace nice."

Jamie's heartbeat raced a little. "That sounds

like… a date."

Stephen smiled. "Good, because that's exactly what it is. I'm going to do things properly. So have yourself ready by six-thirty. That's what time the taxi will be here."

"Taxi?" This was getting better.

Stephen gave an emphatic nod. "Yup. Dinner is already booked too."

He leaned back in his chair. "You must have felt pretty confident I'd say yes."

"Then you *are* saying yes?" Stephen's gaze was locked on his.

Jamie breathed a little easier. "I'd love to go on a date with you." When Stephen let out an obvious sigh of relief, Jamie's heart gave a flutter. *This obviously means a lot to him.*

Jamie couldn't wait to see what the evening would bring.

Then he grinned. "Me first in the bathroom," he called out as Stephen went to collect his bag.

Stephen laughed. "I thought that was a house rule. The able-bodied get to wait their turn, right?"

"Damn straight." Jamie shut down the program he was working on. It wasn't as if he could concentrate anyhow. *I'm going on a date. With Stephen.*

If he could survive that long, because right then he was buzzing, and his pulse was racing.

"So how am I doing?" Stephen whispered as their waiter went away with their cocktail order.

Jamie hadn't stopped smiling since they'd left the house, but he did his best to straighten his features. "Well now, let's see. You booked a taxi that was wheelchair accessible. You chose a restaurant that's also accessible. And on top of that, you've started the evening with cocktails." He couldn't hold back that smile a second longer. "I'd say you were on a roll, so don't blow it." He licked his lips. "I can't wait to try their Espresso Martini."

Stephen frowned. "Wait a minute. I thought you didn't like vodka?"

Jamie gave a shrug. "What can I say? I lied." Then he gave the menu his full attention. He'd never been to the Bostonia Public House, and he liked the look of it. Booths lined the window side of the restaurant, the seats covered in a yellow leather-like fabric that gave the place a sunny feel. There were tall stools at the bar, and single tables for one or two diners in a row along the center of the floor. There was also plenty of room to maneuver, so it got Jamie's vote.

Stephen let out a low moan. "Oh my God. Fork tender meatballs. They sound great."

"They make a *sound*? Do they sing too? Are they part of the live music?"

Stephen lowered his menu and looked Jamie in the eye. "I have *never* been happier to hear you crack a joke."

Jamie smiled. "You should know me by now. It takes a helluva lot to keep me down." He swallowed. "But it's taken me until now to feel more like my usual self."

Stephen sighed. "And that's down to me. We'll talk more later, I promise, but for now, I want to enjoy this moment with you."

Right then the cocktails arrived, and Jamie had to admit Stephen's Blueberry Mojito looked delicious. When the waiter hovered, clearly expecting their order, Jamie rattled off the two dishes that had leaped out at him, and Stephen did the same.

As the waiter walked away, Jamie let out a happy sigh. "Do you know how nice it is to have a waiter actually *talk* to me?"

Stephen frowned. "What do you mean?"

"I've eaten out with my family, and there have been times when a waiter has asked my mom or dad for my order. It was like I didn't exist."

"I can't see that going down well with your parents," Stephen remarked.

He snorted. "It didn't. Mom simply gave him a sweet fake smile and said, 'I really don't have a clue what he wants to order. Why don't you ask him?'"

"Does that happen a lot?"

"Yeah. But I don't think he was being rude on purpose. It's a reflex, I guess. People don't know how to react to a person with a disability, and so they freeze up. If there's an able-bodied person around, that makes it easier for them. But enough talk of waiters." He raised his glass. "Here's to tater tot poutine and lobster mac and cheese."

Stephen raised his glass too. "I've got a better idea. Here's to our first date."

Okay, that made his heartbeat race again. "To

our first date." They clinked glasses, and then he sipped the chilled martini, relishing the rich coffee flavor. When he set his glass down, Jamie relaxed into his chair. "If we make it to a second date, that'll be a first right there."

Stephen stilled. "Wait…"

Jamie nodded. "Yeah, you heard that correctly. I've had lots of first dates. Never gotten a second though." When Stephen's face fell, Jamie reached across and took his hand. "But there *is* going to be a second date, isn't there?" He knew that, from balls to bones.

"And a third. And a fourth."

Jamie grinned. "If you're hoping to get lucky tonight, you're going the right way about it." The waiter approached, and Jamie couldn't resist. As he placed the dishes on the table, Jamie murmured, "Well, if you're buying me dinner, the *least* I can do is sleep with you."

Stephen almost choked on his mojito.

The waiter's eyes were like saucers. Then he grinned, leaned in, and whispered to Stephen, "Looks like this is your lucky night, buddy. And by the way, you have excellent taste." He straightened and walked off with the slightest sashay of his hips.

Stephen gave Jamie a mock glare. "I can't take you anywhere, can I?"

Jamie blew him a kiss. "You love me, and you know it." Then he realized what he'd said, and he froze. He *didn't* know, not for sure. He hoped so.

Stephen apparently took his words in the lighthearted way they'd been uttered. "And I wouldn't change you, not for anything."

Jamie took refuge in his starter. From the moment he'd seen the book cover on Stephen's Kindle, hope blossomed inside him, swelling into a flood of optimism and expectation. Their date so far was everything he'd dreamed of, and certainly nothing like any other date he'd ever been on. For one thing, he had an idea that this one might actually end up where he wanted it to end—in bed.

I think I've waited long enough, don't you, Lord? What do I have to do to make this a night to remember?

And here he was again, making bargains with the Almighty.

"Jamie."

He gave a start. Stephen was grinning at him. "Our server wants to know if you'd like dessert."

Jamie jerked his head in the direction of their decidedly cute waiter, who merely gazed at him with twinkling eyes, as if he knew exactly what had been going on in Jamie's head.

Jamie coughed and peered at the menu. He wasn't even sure he had room for a dessert, not after tater tots and lobster mac and cheese. He did *not* want to feel stuffed later on, especially if—

Nope. Don't go counting any chickens, okay?

"I think I'll pass," he said, giving the waiter a polite smile. The waiter gave him a knowing smile in return, and Jamie had never felt so *seen*. Stephen asked for the check, and Jamie finished his glass of Sauvignon Blanc. It had been a perfect dinner, and now he was excited to see what happened when they got home.

"Ready to go?"

Jamie gave him a wide smile. "Yeah. This has been a wonderful evening."

"And it's not over yet." When Jamie arched his eyebrows, Stephen grinned, his eyes gleaming. "Well, I bought you dinner, so the *least* you can do is sleep with me."

Jamie caught his breath. "If you call for a taxi, how fast can it get here?"

That grin hadn't slipped. "I ordered it on my phone fifteen minutes ago. It's waiting for us outside the door."

"Then why are you standing there talking to me?" Jamie backed away from the table and headed for the door, Stephen following.

He was still chuckling when he wheeled Jamie up the metal ramp into the taxi.

Jamie wasn't laughing. He was too busy mentally planning what he was going to do when he got through his front door.

This was going to be as perfect an experience as he could make it.

K.C. Wells

Chapter Twenty

As soon as Stephen closed the door behind them, Jamie went into hyper mode.

"Okay, I need to take a shower, so if you want the bathroom, now's the time. And then I need to—"

Stephen stopped his words with a gentle finger against Jamie's lips. "Jamie? The only thing you need to do right this second is take a breath—and kiss me." He removed his finger and bent down. Jamie tilted his head back, and Stephen claimed his mouth in a sweet, chaste kiss, his palm curved around Jamie's cheek.

Finally.

His lips were warm and soft, and Jamie wanted more of them. He reached out with both arms, looped them around Stephen's neck, and returned the kiss, their lips locked, Jamie's eyes wide open because he was not going to miss *one fucking second* of this. Because this was wonderful.

When they parted, Stephen murmured, "For the record? If I wore glasses, right now they'd be steamed up."

Jamie grinned. "You sure know how to make a guy feel good. And it's nice to know I've still got it." Jamie forced himself to sit back in his chair. He looked into Stephen's eyes. "While I could spend all day kissing you, there are things we need to discuss before we do anything, okay? I'm not trying to put a dampener on the mood, or heaven forbid, kill it stone dead, but yeah, a little communication needs to take place." He knew by heart what he wanted to say, and he was *finally* getting to say it.

"Let's go to your room while we talk?"

Jamie could do that. He wheeled into his bedroom and waited until Stephen was seated on the edge of the bed. He was surprised to find his hands shaking a little.

Stephen noticed. He leaned forward and took Jamie's hands in his. "Okay. Before you get going, shall I tell you what I already know?"

Jamie nodded, his throat suddenly tight.

"The most important thing is… you're beautiful and I want you. Got that?"

Jamie shivered. "Dude, what a way to start. Yeah, I got it. I want you too."

Stephen closed the gap between them and kissed him again, only this time he parted Jamie's lips with his tongue, and Jamie goddamn *melted*. He gave as good as he got, until Stephen was feeding him soft noises of arousal, and Jamie was *dying* to get their clothes off.

Stephen broke the kiss, his breathing erratic. "Whoa there. I think you said something about communication?"

"We *are* communicating." Jamie grinned. "We're speaking in tongues."

Stephen snorted. "Somehow I don't think that's what the Bible meant." He sat back, Jamie's hands still in his. "Okay, let's talk erections. You said you get them. I'm guessing you need stimulation to achieve one, seeing as you said your injury was at T10, so that means you can't get erect thinking about me naked." His lips twitched. "And you *have* been thinking about me naked, haven't you?"

Jamie chuckled. "I don't know whether to whack you on the arm for being a smug bastard, or say *Duh* and give you an eye roll. And how in the hell do you know about—?" Then it hit him. "You really *did* do some research last night."

Stephen nodded. "I said I wanted to learn, didn't I? So I did my homework. These toys you mentioned? Will any of them do the trick?"

Jamie thought instantly of his vibrator. "Definitely." He bit his lip. "Although I *can* think of at least one other method of stimulation that doesn't require toys." His gaze flickered down to Stephen's mouth, then back up to his eyes.

Stephen's cheeks flushed. "Funny. I was thinking the same thing." He focused his gaze on Jamie's lips, and warmth flooded through him. "I'm also guessing you'll need to get yourself ready. That's okay. You take as much time as you need. Now, do you have a wedge, or something else like that, in case we get that far tonight? If you don't, we'll use pillows until I can get one."

Holy fuck. This gets better and better.

"I have one," Jamie blurted out. "It's on a shelf in my closet. It's still in its original packaging." And didn't *that* say a lot? Then Stephen's words registered. "Hey. In *case* we get that far?"

Stephen stroked his cheek. "Cool your jets. I'm thinking we go slow. That okay with you?" His eyes were warm. "I'm in no rush."

"Sure, but *you* haven't been thinking about getting laid since 2011. I wanna make up for lost time."

Stephen laughed. "Well, you're not going to do that all in one night, okay?"

"Spoilsport," Jamie muttered. Not that he meant it. The idea of them taking things nice and slow sent more warmth spreading through his body.

"Is there anything I can do? Put on some music? What would you like?"

"Heavy rock always does it for me," Jamie said with a straight face. When Stephen laughed, Jamie squeezed his hands. "Wow. I'm impressed. Seriously, where have you *been* all my life?"

"In California," Stephen said simply. "But I'm here now, and I'm not going anywhere." He moved slowly, his hand gentle on Jamie's neck as they kissed, taking his time.

"Newsflash," Jamie murmured. Stephen pulled back to gaze at him, and Jamie smiled. "If I wore glasses, they'd be steamed up too."

"Good to know." Stephen cleared his throat. "Okay. What do you like? What do you enjoy?" His eyes sparkled. "Tell me where to touch you, to make you feel good."

"I will, when we're both naked, but look…" It didn't matter that Stephen had taken the time to research the intricacies of sex and disability. The last thing Jamie wanted to do was disappoint him.

Stephen squeezed his hands once more. "Do you watch porn?" Jamie nodded. "Well, me too, so I think I'd better say this now." He paused. "Don't go expecting any porn star athletics from me, okay?"

Jamie laughed, and the tension across his back and shoulders dissipated. "Thanks for letting me know." This was a huge deal, and Stephen was saying *all* the right things.

"And I suppose this is where I should mention expectations."

That got his interest. "I'm listening."

Stephen coughed. "The thing is... what I read last night... well, it said there are things you can do to prolong your erections, so I was wondering..."

Okay, there was only one direction this could be going in.

Jamie took a breath. "What you read was correct. My erections don't last that long, but we can stave off the inevitable by using a cock ring and... Viagra. But if we're gonna do that, you gotta give me notice, because apparently it takes a while to kick in. So to speak." He gave Stephen a speculative glance. "Tell me if I'm reading this all wrong, but I sorta get the impression you want me to—"

"Yes, I do. If that's okay."

Jamie gave a slow grin. "Please tell me we're done communicating?" Because all he wanted right then was to be balls deep in Stephen's ass.

Apparently, they were going to take their time getting there.

"We're done. For now." Stephen cupped his chin and locked gazes with him. "But if you want to ask something, or stop at any time, you just have to say so, okay?"

Tears pricked the corners of his eyes, and Stephen gently wiped them away with his thumbs. Jamie pushed out a wry chuckle. "You are amazing. In twenty-four hours, I've gone from wanting to kick you out of the house to never wanting you to leave."

"I had to do *something*, right? I couldn't lose you." Stephen kissed his forehead. "I was an idiot for not educating myself in the first place."

"Hey, we got there in the end."

Stephen's eyes danced with amusement. "We're not there yet. And we won't get there if *someone* doesn't get his ass into that bathroom and do what a boy's gotta do."

"And *someone's* impatient." A thought struck him. He reached into his pocket, removed his phone, and tossed it onto the bed. "Look in Music. There's a playlist called Mood stuff. That might be what you had in mind, in case you didn't like the heavy rock idea." Then he coughed. "Sorry, but I need my bed to get out of these clothes. And while I *love* the idea of doing a striptease for you, I'd rather save the big reveal for when I come out of the bathroom, okay?"

Despite his jokes and witty comeback, Jamie was nervous as hell.

Stephen got up off the bed and headed for the door. "I've already seen what you're about to reveal. Well, most of it. You were hiding something under a towel, I recall." He came back to Jamie's chair and bent down. Jamie shivered again as warm lips brushed against his ear. "And I can't wait to see it." Then he was gone.

In all the time Jamie had been using the wheelchair, he'd never gotten out of it in such a hurry. Except for that time when he fell out of it, and he wasn't counting *that*.

Jamie looked at his reflection in the mirror over the sink. His heart hammered and his pulse raced.

Well, I'm as ready as I'll ever be.

He left the bathroom and went along the hallway into his room. As he pushed open the door, he caught his breath.

Oh, Stephen.

There were candles *everywhere*, giving off a wonderful aroma of vanilla and sandalwood that was just right. They gave the room a beautiful glow. 'Fade Into You' by Mazzy Star filled the air with the sound of a guitar, and her voice was freaking perfect. A large bottle of lube stood on the nightstand, a box of condoms next to it. Stephen had spread a towel over the comforter.

Dear Lord, look *at him.*

Stephen lay on the bed, naked as a jay bird, lazily playing with his dick. He smiled as Jamie rolled toward the bed. "Do you want to get on here under your own steam, or can I help? I could lift you onto the bed, if that's okay."

Jamie chuckled. "Much as I love the idea of you lifting me—and don't think I don't appreciate the romance of it all—I wouldn't want you to… strain anything. That would sort of defeat the object of the night, don't you think?" He smiled. "But thanks for asking." He parked the chair next to the bed, and transferred onto it. He centered himself on the towel and lay on his back, his stomach churning and his #

chest tightening.

Stephen was there in a heartbeat, his hand on Jamie's chest, stroking it slowly. "Hey there, gorgeous."

"You're doing great things for my ego."

Stephen cupped his cheek. "If no guy you've ever dated has told you that, you've been dating the wrong guys." He gazed at Jamie's body. "Nice reveal, by the way."

Jamie expelled a breath. He'd been tempted to jerk off a little in the shower, so that he at least had a hard on when he came into the room. Then he reconsidered.

Let him see me as I am. Then let him see what he does to me when he touches me.

"Comfortable?" When Jamie nodded, he leaned over and kissed Jamie on the lips, and Jamie sighed into the kiss. He cupped Stephen's nape and pulled him in, deepening the kiss, allowing himself to relax beneath Stephen's gentle hand.

When he pulled back, Jamie expelled a long breath. "It's like being at a buffet. I don't know where to start. There's too much to touch and taste."

Stephen bent his head over Jamie's chest, his breath warming it. "Well, I'd like a lesson in what turns Jamie on." When his lips brushed over Jamie's nipple, Jamie groaned. "Bingo." Stephen lifted his chin and grinned. "And so the hunt begins."

"W-what are you hunting for?" Jamie's breathing hitched as Stephen tugged gently on his nipple with his teeth.

Stephen's eyes gleamed. "Erogenous zones."

His heartbeat went into overdrive.

When Mazzy Star finished and Aretha Franklin took over with 'Do Right Woman, Do Right Man', Jamie submerged himself in a world of sensation. He lost all track of time as Stephen kissed, licked, nipped and teased his chest, nipples, belly, shoulders… The lightest trace of a finger over his abs sent shivers rippling through him.

Words were few, but then they weren't needed much beyond 'Like that?' and 'Again,' 'There,' and quite a few calls on the Lord. Stephen kissed his pits, and Jamie shuddered at the new sensation. *How come I didn't know that felt so goddamn good?* He lay there while Stephen worshipped his body, his skin tingling with each and every touch. Now and again Stephen alternated his sensual exploration with kisses that made Jamie's head spin and his heart pound. Then it was back to exploring.

Jamie had never been so turned on, and Stephen hadn't even laid a finger on his dick.

He's gonna get there eventually, right?

"You're doing all the work," Jamie murmured as Stephen circled his navel with his tongue. "Oh Lord, that feels amazing." He hoped the Lord didn't mind the circumstances. *Why should He? Didn't His dad invent sex in the first place?*

Stephen inclined his face toward Jamie. "But I'm enjoying the work immensely. Besides, you've been waiting since 2011 for this, right? *You* get to play another time. Tonight is all about me pleasuring you." He shifted lower, until his lips were inches from Jamie's soft cock that lay against his thigh. "Although… this is going to give me no small amount of pleasure too. Can't tell you how much I've wanted to do this." And then he licked the head.

Sweet Jesus, watching him was amazing.

Jamie couldn't tear his gaze away from the sight of Stephen taking his dick into his mouth. His heartbeat slipped into high gear as Stephen bobbed up and down on his cock, taking him deeper with each pass, until Stephen's nose was buried in Jamie's pubes, and his shaft was surrounded by warmth. Jamie stroked Stephen's hair, his breath leaving him in short staccato bursts as he watched his cock lengthen and thicken, Stephen's fingers curled around its base.

"Oh... oh yeah..." Words eluded him as he drowned in an ocean of arousal, his skin tingling, heart beating fast, goose bumps breaking out all over his arms and chest, pebbling his nipples. Jamie tweaked them, the tingling increasing as he was swept closer to his orgasm. And when he came, it felt like every sensation was heightened, sending shudders of pleasure through him.

Stephen slowly pulled free of his cock and shifted on the bed to lie beside him. "I like how you taste."

Jamie pulled him into a deep kiss, his arms around Stephen as he clung to him, his heartbeat gradually returning to its normal rhythm. "That was..." He swallowed. No words could possibly encompass the emotions and thoughts that overwhelmed him right then.

"I have to ask something."

Jamie gave him a quizzical glance. "Ask."

"Was that your first blow job since the accident?"

"Seeing as I can't blow myself? Yeah. And before you ask, it felt awesome." Except awesome really didn't cut it. He only had the one blow job with Reece to go on, and that had been over in a heartbeat, but with Stephen, it had been so much more.

See what happens when emotions are connected too?

"So how do I rate on a score of #1 to #10?"

Jamie could easily become addicted to that sated feeling of warmth and sheer contentment. "You're at least a #12." Stephen sighed happily, and the sound sent Jamie's spirits soaring. *Looks like both of us are happy.*

Stephen's smile faltered, and Jamie lifted his chin with his fingers. "What is it?"

"It's late, and I have work in the morning. I know I said we wouldn't get to do everything in one night, and that was me being sensible. But…"

"But?"

Stephen kissed him, a slow, lingering kiss that made him feel lightheaded. "I don't want tonight to end."

Jamie's breathing quickened. "Then don't let it. Stay with me."

He blinked. "Really?"

Jamie laughed. "Yes, really. I don't hog the sheets because I don't move around when I sleep. I don't snore—at least, I don't *think* I do." He caressed Stephen's cheek. "And I'd love to wake up to you next to me."

"I'd love that too." Stephen sat up. "Is there anything you'd like me to do?"

He grinned. "Yes. You can blow out all these

candles." He glanced at the nightstand where the bottle of lube stood next to the condoms. "We'll get to use those another day."

"I'm thinking tomorrow."

Jamie chuckled. "I love the way you think." As Stephen got up off the bed and went around the room, blowing out the flames, Jamie watched him, admiring his lean body and firm ass. What occupied his thoughts, however, was all the care and attention Stephen had shown throughout the evening.

At some point between Stephen turning up at Horn Pond and the last few hours they'd spent together, Jamie had fallen in love. He couldn't pinpoint the exact moment, and he didn't care. He knew he didn't want this to end.

He also knew he had no worries about there not being a second date. What *did* cross his mind was how long he was going to leave it before he told Stephen how he truly felt.

He couldn't be so caring and considerate if he didn't love me a little, right? Except Jamie didn't want a little of Stephen's love.

He wanted it all.

Chapter Twenty-One

Stephen opened his eyes at the sound of the alarm on his phone. He didn't want to move. He was warm and snug. Then he realized the warmth might have been due to the body occupying the other side of the bed.

That brought a smile. It had been a while since he'd spent the night with someone, and he'd slept soundly.

"This is so unfair."

Stephen rolled onto his side to face Jamie. "And good morning to you too. What's unfair?" Jamie looked adorable with his black hair ruffled and the faintest shadow of a beard.

"You. How *dare* you wake up looking so freaking gorgeous? Even your bed hair is cute."

Stephen chuckled. "Newsflash. I thought the same thing about you the other day. You were asleep, and all I wanted to do was stroke your cheek."

"Why didn't you? I'd have liked that." Jamie bit his lip. "And it's not your *cheek* I wanna stroke this morning." He propped himself up on his elbow and peered down to where Stephen's morning wood was tenting the sheets. Stephen couldn't resist jerking it a little, and Jamie groaned. "Good Lord, your dick did push-ups." He gazed at Stephen with wide eyes. "Can I say good morning to it?" He licked his lips.

Stephen laughed. "Forget it. Work, remember?"

Jamie's eyes sparkled. "I can bring you off in less than five minutes. Time me."

"No. I'll be late." God, but it was a tempting prospect.

"But you can't ignore it. I mean, *look* at it."

Stephen gave him a mock glare. "I'll survive."

Jamie let out a theatrical gasp. "You'd deny me my first blow job since—"

"Oh, for God's sake." Stephen threw back the sheets, revealing his heavy shaft that stood upright. "There. It's all yours. Have at it." Not that he was all *that* averse to a morning blow job.

So what if I'm a little late?

Jamie grinned as he pulled himself into an upright position. "Then get your ass over here. Sit astride me and hold on."

Stephen straddled Jamie, his cock brushing against Jamie's lips. "Hold onto wha—Holy *fuck*!" His shaft was engulfed in wet heat. Stephen couldn't help himself. He gripped the headboard and rocked his hips back and forth, keeping his thrusts shallow as he filled Jamie's mouth. Judging by the moans that poured from Jamie's lips, he was enjoying the experience every bit as much as Stephen was.

"You like that?" Stephen murmured. "You like having my dick in your mouth?"

Jamie's eye roll convinced him the sound he'd heard was the word *Duh*. Jamie grabbed his ass and squeezed hard, propelling him forward, pushing him deeper.

Shit. He wasn't even going to last *two* minutes,

let alone five.

Stephen came with a groan, shooting his load into Jamie's mouth, his hands cradling Jamie's head as his cock pulsed out the final drops. Stephen let go to grasp his shaft with one hand and rub the head against Jamie's lower lip, Jamie's tongue darting out to lick it unhurriedly.

Stephen's legs trembled and he shuddered, his body tingling. "Wow."

Jamie beamed up at him. "I take it that's a good wow."

Stephen bent down to kiss him, tasting his own spunk there. "Now *that's* the way to wake me up. I only wish we had time for more." Another soft kiss. "Later, okay?"

Jamie's eyes shone. "I'll be thinking about you while you're gone."

That was all the incentive Stephen needed to get his ass out of the office ASAP when work was done. "Can't wait to see you tonight."

"Well, there's stuff that needs to happen before tonight swings around, the first thing being me in the bathroom, pronto."

"I've got to get ready for work!" Stephen protested.

"Sorry, but *my* catheter beats *your* shower."

There was no way Stephen was going to argue with that. "It's all yours," he said, shifting so Jamie could get to his chair. "Why didn't you say something?"

"I couldn't," Jamie called out as he wheeled toward the door. "I had my mouth full."

Stephen chuckled. He could see a lot of late

mornings in his future.

I'm going to have to set my alarm half an hour earlier.

Dad walked into Stephen's office, closed the door, and sat facing his desk.

That was *never* a good thing.

Stephen closed the file he was working on and gave Dad his full attention. "What's up?"

"I was about to ask you the same question. What's wrong with you? You were bad enough yesterday, but today is worse."

Stephen frowned. "Who says there's anything wrong?"

Dad snorted. "Every time I've stuck my head around your door, you've been distracted. You didn't even notice me, I'll bet."

Stephen's stomach clenched. *Not once.* He straightened in his chair. "I'm sorry. You're right. I've had something on my mind." Yeah, he had—Jamie. Maybe it was because everything between them was so new, but he hadn't been able to keep his mind on his work.

He couldn't wait to get home to Jamie.

"Stephen?"

God, he was doing it again.

Dad shook his head. "I don't know where your head takes you, but it's obviously more interesting than here." Then his expression softened. "Am I working you too hard? Is that it? Neither of us have stopped since we opened, and you were working right up until we left California."

"I'm only working as hard as you are."

Dad nodded. "Well, maybe you should take a break. Go away someplace. Relax."

Stephen stared at him with wide eyes. "Okay, who are you, and what have you done with my dad?" Take a *break*?

Dad cackled. "Am I that much of a taskmaster? Seriously, son, you've earned a break. But *after* that? We work like Trojans until the holidays, you got that?"

"I got it." Then Stephen recalled Jamie's words from the other day. He'd mentioned taking a vacation.

An idea began to dawn. A perfectly *wonderful* idea.

"Stephen?"

He gave a start. "Sir?"

Dad chuckled. "I think you were already off someplace, planning a trip. You think you could do that on your own time?"

"Yes, sir."

Dad got up from his chair. "Let me know what you decide." And with that, he left the office.

Stephen picked up his phone and scrolled through his contacts.

He had a trip to plan.

"Jamie? You got a minute?" Stephen called out as he closed the front door behind him.

"For you? Several," Jamie hollered back from the living room. "There's beer in the refrigerator. I went shopping."

Stephen shucked off his jacket. "I hope you didn't buy too many groceries." He went into the kitchen and opened the fridge. Not too many, thankfully.

Jamie rolled into the room. "Now you've got me intrigued."

Stephen got out two bottles of beer and opened them. He handed one to Jamie, and they clinked. "I have a surprise for you." He hoped to God Jamie liked the idea.

Jamie took a drink, then gave Stephen a quizzical glance. "Out with it. What are you up to?"

"Remember the other day, when you said you were thinking of taking a short vacation?" Stephen took another drink. "Well… how does a week in Florida grab you?"

Jamie frowned. "Huh?"

"You heard right. A week in Florida. Leaving Saturday. Our accommodation is already booked. I only have to finalize the flights."

"You booked accommodation… before you even asked me?" Then Jamie widened his eyes. "Your grandma."

Stephen nodded, excitement bubbling up inside him at the look of joy on Jamie's face. "She can't wait for us to visit. So… what do you say? We both need this."

Jamie arched his eyebrows. "Have you cleared

it with your dad?"

"Hell, it was his idea." Jamie didn't need to know about the rest of the conversation, when Stephen shared his plans.

"Are you going to drive down?"

Stephen shook his head. "We'll fly."

Dad stilled. "We?"

"Sure. I'm taking Jamie with me."

Dad frowned. "Why? Isn't that going to complicate the trip? I mean, there's enough rigmarole about getting on a plane these days, without adding a disabled passenger. There's a load of things you need to sort out with the airline before he can even board the plane. And what about his wheelchair?"

God, there was so much Stephen ached to say about the insensitivity his dad was displaying, but he bit his tongue.

He took a deep breath. "I've already checked with the airline. I have to tell them when I book the flights. And Dad?" Stephen looked him in the eye. "I don't see Jamie as a complication, okay?"

His dad had the grace to look sheepish. "Okay. It's your vacation, after all."

"Stephen?"

He snapped to. Jamie was grinning at him. "You're already imagining yourself on a beach, aren't you?"

"You got me." Better to let him think that. "So you like the idea?"

"Like it? I *love* it." Jamie wheeled himself out of the kitchen.

"Where are you going?" Stephen called after

him.

"To start packing. I need to figure out what I'm taking."

"We've got days yet." Stephen smiled to himself. Jamie was such a big kid. Then he realized Jamie's excitement was infectious. *Maybe I need to start packing too.*

Jamie was in heaven. Stephen was spooned around him, his arms enveloping him. *I never want to sleep alone ever again.*

"What are you thinking?" Stephen sounded drowsy. Not all that surprising, given the lateness of the hour.

"About the way things turned out."

"Happy?" Stephen kissed the back of his neck, and Jamie shivered.

"Yeah. But you keep on doing that, and I'll be even happier."

Gentle fingers trailed down his arm, and goose bumps followed them. "Can I ask you something?"

Jamie sighed. "The mood I'm in right now? You could ask me anything."

"There's something I don't get. You're smart. Gorgeous. Talented. Sexy."

Jamie chuckled. "Ooh, keep going, you're on a roll."

"Doof. I guess what I'm asking is, how come you haven't been on that many dates?"

He sighed. "But I *have* been on lots of dates. The only trouble was, like I said before, they were all first dates, and probably nothing like *yours* were." *Jesus, how do I explain this?* "We all know how a first date *should* go, right? That look across the dinner table? The one that tells you they're into you? They want you? And then there are the dates from hell. The ones where you can't wait to get out of there."

He paused, his mind going over the awkward silences, the glances, the stilted conversations. "We've all had dates like that, right? Well, imagine if every date was like that. Where it doesn't take you long to realize they asked you out because of curiosity. 'Ooh, what's it like to date a disabled guy?' And not one of them wanted a second date. Maybe they were picturing what my legs looked like without my best jeans. Did they think I was all mangled and deformed under there? Because all they had to do was ask, and I'd have dropped trou in a heartbeat."

"They have no idea what they missed out on," Stephen said softly. "A beautiful man, inside and out."

"You like my outside, huh?" Jamie joked, pushing away the memories because he didn't want that pain in his head. Then he gasped as Stephen slid his hand lower, until his fingers were between Jamie's ass cheeks.

"The inside might feel pretty good."

Jamie's breathing quickened, his heart pounding. Another first right there. "You want to? I mean, it's late. You're not on vacation yet. We—"

Stephen rolled him onto his back, and then Jamie sighed as he was pinned to the bed. "Do you want me inside you?"

Jamie managed an eye roll. "That's a rhetorical question, right?"

Stephen chuckled. "Funny man."

Jamie locked his arms around Stephen's neck. "Of course I want you inside me. But we might need some props."

Stephen kissed the tip of his nose. "I'm on it. Get the lube." He regarded Jamie closely. "Are we good to go, or do you need to—"

"We're good," Jamie assured him. "Now go get the wedge from the closet." Christ, his heart was beating fast.

As Stephen got out of bed and walked around it, Jamie glanced at his crotch, where his dick was already stiffening. "In case you're interested, I think you'd give Reece a run for his money." Stephen wasn't as long, thank God, but he sure was thicker.

We're gonna need a lot of lube.

"Ready?"

Jamie gazed up at him. "Do I look ready?" His ankles rested on Stephen's shoulders, his ass on the wedge at the edge of the bed. Stephen stood between his legs, his cock encased in latex, glistening with lube.

Stephen smiled. "You look amazing." Then he leaned over, until Jamie's knees were almost at his ears, and kissed him. Jamie grabbed hold of Stephen's head and pulled him in for a deeper kiss, pouring into it all the longing and need that raged inside him.

"Now," he murmured against Stephen's lips. Jamie loved the look of awe as Stephen slowly inched his way into Jamie's body, until flesh met flesh, and Stephen was home.

"Oh dear God," Stephen groaned. "The way you *feel…*"

The way he looks….

They shared kiss after kiss, never once losing that connection as Stephen moved in and out of him, maintaining a steady pace, stroking Jamie's chest with one hand while the other worked his dick.

"Talk to me," Jamie demanded, needing to hear his voice.

Stephen's face was inches from his. "Do you want to know how goddamn good your body feels on my cock?" In and out, so goddamn slowly. "How much I love it that you're hard in my hand?" In. Out. "How much those little noises you make turn me on?" Those gorgeous blue-green eyes, locked on his. "How I only have to look at you to know you're loving this *every damn bit* as much as I am?"

"Yes," he whispered, his fingers tugging gently on the mat of hair that covered Stephen's chest, loving the feel of it. "More."

Stephen kissed him, only now with more heat, more fervor, as he quickened the pace. "How's that for more?" he gasped out between kisses.

Jamie nodded, unable to look away as Stephen cupped Jamie's face between his hands, hips pumping, while Jamie's heart beat faster still. Wherever Stephen kissed on his body, he left a trail of goose bumps, as though every inch of skin on Jamie's arms and chest had become one huge erogenous zone. He pushed out soft cries as Stephen sped up, knowing they were close. And when Stephen stiffened, his dick buried to the hilt, Jamie came, tears pricking his eyes at the moans of pleasure that fell from Stephen's lips, the look in his eyes as he scooped up what little spunk there was, and brought it to his lips.

Then Stephen was in his arms once more, his lips on Jamie's, tremors rippling through him, matching the shivers that coursed through Jamie's body.

Jamie let out a long, happy sigh. "Dear Lord, it's *so* much better without the tree bark."

Chapter Twenty-Two

Stephen let out a happy sigh as the taxi sped away from the airport. "God, I've missed this." The sky was so blue, it hurt his eyes to look at it. The temperature had to be around the high seventies. Just right. Certainly nothing like the chill in Boston right then.

Jamie laughed. "Aw, have you been having withdrawal symptoms? You been missing the sunshine and heat of California?"

"Yes!"

"Well, there *is* a solution. In the summer, you go see Marie and the kids. And any other time you want to go there." Jamie grinned. "I'll go too, of course."

Stephen narrowed his gaze. "Let me guess. Water skiing."

He laughed. "You know me far too well." Jamie gazed through the window at the passing scenery. "We could vacation here too. There's a thriving gay community in Fort Lauderdale."

"Why would I want to hang around other gay guys? Been there, done that, got—"

Jamie swiftly reached forward and silenced him with a finger to his lips. "No," he said quietly. "That life is over. And not *all* gay men are like the assholes you dated, okay?" He removed his hand. "One day I'll take you back to Cali to prove it."

Stephen huffed. "Why on earth would I want to go back there?"

"Maybe one day you should, to slay those demons that still mess with your mind." Jamie regarded him thoughtfully. "Are you ever going to tell me what happened to you?"

"Nope." Stephen patted his knee. "Trust me, you don't want to know. You'd only get mad, or upset, or vengeful, or all three, and that's not you, baby. So stay my sunshine Jamie, okay?"

Jamie smiled. "Yeah, I can do that."

The taxi pulled up outside the house, and Stephen paid the driver, who then got out to set up the ramp for Jamie. The front door opened as Jamie extricated himself from the taxi's innards, and Grandma stood there, beaming.

"I was checking online to see if your flight arrived on time," she said as Stephen made a beeline for her, dropping the bags on her driveway. She held her arms wide, craning her neck to gaze up at him. "My goodness, I swear you're even taller than last time I saw you." She gave him a fierce hug.

"Grandma, that was only three years ago, and I haven't grown since then." He bit back a smile. "I think you've shrunk though." Her hair was a little whiter, and she was wearing it shorter than he remembered, but other than that, she'd changed little.

"Sadly, that's true. I've lost an inch and a half since then. They're around here someplace." Her eyes twinkled. "So if you happen to come across them during your stay, tell them I want them back."

"And I want my hug," Jamie demanded, rolling

toward her. The taxi had already left.

She stared at him with wide eyes, then swallowed hard. "Oh my. Look at you." She let go of Stephen and went over to him, slipping her arms around his shoulders. "It's been so long." Grandma tilted his chin and gazed into his eyes. "*There's the* Jamie I remember. My laughing boy."

Stephen didn't miss the sparkle at the corner of Jamie's eyes. "It's good to see you too, Mrs. Welch."

Grandma frowned as she stepped back. "Last time I saw you, it was *Grandma*, I do recall. So we'll have none of that Mrs. Welch business. I've got your rooms ready, and you're sharing a bathroom, though I don't suppose you'll mind, seeing as you already share a house."

Stephen did *not* intend sleeping in his own bed, but that wasn't something to share with his grandma. He glanced toward the house. "Only one step. That's easy enough to manage."

Jamie nodded. "And I could use the bathroom right about now."

Grandma stood aside. "Then let's get you inside. I've got lunch ready for you, and then after, we can sit out by the pool."

Jamie grinned. "Awesome. I brought my bathing suit with me."

Stephen rolled his eyes. "Wait till you see it, Grandma. It's got pictures of donuts all over it."

"And what's wrong with that?" she retorted. She watched as Stephen backed Jamie's wheelchair up the step and into the house. Stephen went out to collect the bags, in time to find Grandma trying to lift Jamie's.

"Hey, leave that. I'll do it." He grabbed them both. "Though I have no idea what he's packed. Did you really need a bag this size for a *week*?" he called into the house.

"Yes. And don't open it."

Stephen shook his head, chuckling.

Grandma followed him into the house. "You two picked a great time to come visit. There's a 5K Walk and Run on Deerfield Beach tomorrow, in aid of the Boys and Girls Clubs of Broward County."

"Is there a 5K *roll*? Because otherwise, I might sit that one out." Jamie said with a smile.

"There's a Harvest Festival at Flamingo Gardens tomorrow, if you wanted a more sedate activity." Her eyes sparkled. "Though I don't think *either* of you would be *remotely* interested in the Oktoberfest that starts next Saturday."

Stephen grinned. "Bratwurst, schnitzel, and strudel—oh my!"

"*You* can eat the bratwurst—*I'll* have the lager and ale." Jamie addressed Grandma with a straight face. "Yeah, you're right, we'd hate that."

She laughed. "You haven't changed, have you?" She pointed to two doors. "Here are your rooms. No fighting over who gets which. Sort it out peacefully, please. I'll have lunch waiting by the time you've unpacked." Then she left them to it.

Stephen pushed open the nearest door and went in, heading for the bed to deposit the bags. "The bathroom is in between with two connecting doors, if I remember. I'd better check it out." He walked over and peered inside, then stilled. "Aw, Grandma." His chest swelled with love.

"What is it?" Jamie wheeled himself over to peek around the door. "Oh, she didn't. That sweet lady."

Straddling the tub was a transfer bench, like the one Jamie had at home, and a commode with a drop-down arm sat over the toilet.

"She didn't need to go to all this trouble," Stephen exclaimed.

"It wasn't all *that* much trouble," came Grandma's voice from behind him. She came into the room and stood next to Jamie's chair. "They're really easy to rent around here. Do you have any idea how many senior citizens there are in Fort Lauderdale?"

Jamie grabbed her hand and kissed it. "It's still a sweet thing to do. Thank you." He squeezed it. "*Now* I see who Stephen gets it from."

"Gets what, sweetheart?"

He smiled. "His consideration for others. The way he cares for people. How he treats them."

She kissed the top of his head. "I would hope everyone has those qualities in them." She patted Stephen's arm, then walked out of the room.

"I love your grandma," Jamie said with a sigh. Then he peered at the room. "Are the beds the same size?"

"I'll check." Stephen grinned. "If one's bigger, you can have it."

"As long as I won't be on my own in it," he said in a low voice.

"You can count on that." Stephen bent down and kissed him, not bothering to keep it chaste.

"Damn," Jamie murmured against his lips. "Is it bedtime yet?"

Stephen chuckled. "Hey, at least you get to see me in my Speedos before then."

Jamie's eyes widened. "You brought a pair of *Speedos*? What are you trying to do, *torture* me?"

Stephen nodded gleefully. "I'm going to lie there by the pool," he whispered, "thinking about sliding my dick into you, and you're going to know *exactly* when I'm thinking it, because I will be so fucking *hard*. Then I'll go for a swim, and when I get out, the fabric will be almost transparent, clinging to my boner, and—"

Jamie gasped. "You bastard. You fucking *tease*."

Stephen wagged his finger. "Uh-uh. Not in Grandma's house, please. Because she *will* wash your mouth out with soap, remember?" *He* sure hadn't forgotten. Stephen gazed innocently at Jamie. "Didn't you want to use the bathroom?"

Jamie made a noise that sounded like a low growl. "I'll deal with you later." He wheeled past Stephen to the bed, fumbled through his bag till he found the container with all his paraphernalia in, then went into the bathroom and closed the door.

"Ooh, I'm really scared," Stephen called through it.

"*How* old are you?" Jamie yelled. "Now go away. I'm… busy."

Stephen left him to it, and set about unpacking their bags. He felt lighter than he had done in ages, and that was down to the prospect of spending a week in the sun with Jamie, with no work to get up for, and all night long to make love.

As long as they kept the noise down.

He grabbed the bags and placed them on the bed. Jamie's was open, and Stephen couldn't help smiling as he peered inside.

I wonder what TSA made of his wedge when it went through the baggage scanner?

"Come *on*," Jamie urged. "I don't know how much longer this'll last." He kept an ear toward the door, convinced Grandma was about to hammer on it at any second, demanding they keep the noise down. *As long as she doesn't come in.* Jamie didn't think she needed that sort of an education, especially at one in the morning.

"I'm doing it, okay? But this is tricky." Stephen had already gotten his feet through, so all he had to do was straddle Jamie, bracing his feet on the bed behind his chair. "What's this position called again?" he whispered.

"Sitting Pretzel." He tugged on his dick, doing his best to keep it firm. *Hold on there. Just stay hard enough to get inside him.* There was no way they were going to wait for Viagra to work, but at least he had the cock ring, which helped some. He had to be in Stephen's ass, like *now*.

Stephen grabbed the arms of the chair, holding himself aloft as Jamie guided his cock to his hole. "Now?" he pleaded.

"Now." Jamie pushed out a low groan as Stephen sank down onto his shaft. "Fuck, that feels good." Stephen wrapped his arms around him, their chests pressed together. "Okay, brace your feet on the edge of the bed and get thrusting."

"Fuck. This isn't easy." Stephen moved up and down, and the friction was fantastic, judging by his facial expression.

"Lemme help." Jamie pushed down on the chair arms, lifting himself up to meet Stephen's thrusts. "Always knew that... upper body work would... come in useful." Dammit, Stephen looked too good, his body tight, his eyes locked on Jamie.
"Aw, fuck."

Stephen groaned. "Is it over?"

"As good as." He'd known his erection wouldn't stay the course, but he'd hoped for longer. Jamie clung to Stephen, their lips meeting in a fervent kiss, his dick still inside him. Stephen didn't move to get off of him, but looped his arms around Jamie's neck, their kisses growing more tender.

Then Stephen started laughing, and damn it if Jamie didn't see the funny side too. "Next time? We plan this better."

Stephen cupped his chin. "But it *was* fun."

"And you know what would be even more fun?" Jamie grinned. "Ever been skinny dipping in the middle of the night?"

"Are you kidding? She'll wake up for sure."

"Aw, live a little." Jamie was picturing being in the cool water, Stephen's arms around him as they kissed in the moonlight. He met Stephen's gaze. "I dare ya."

Stephen rolled his eyes. "One of these days, you're gonna say that and I won't rise to it."

"But not tonight," Jamie guessed.

Stephen kissed him, slow and hot. "No, not tonight."

Jamie gave himself up to another kiss, reminding himself how lucky he was to have Stephen in his life.

K.C. Wells

Chapter Twenty-Three

The hardest thing about being around his grandma was keeping his hands off Jamie, Stephen concluded. They sat at her breakfast table, drinking coffee and eating eggs, bacon, sausage, with toasted English muffins, and all Stephen wanted to do was give Jamie's hand a squeeze now and again. He supposed the urge would die off a little as they grew more accustomed to being together, but right then he wanted to touch Jamie. Maybe it was the desire to check this was real.

Grandma cleared her throat. "Something you boys want to tell me?"

Jamie darted a quick glance in his direction, but said nothing.

Stephen gave her a hopefully perplexed look. "Excuse me?"

She wiped her lips with her napkin, then settled back in her chair. "Yes, I'm old. My bones crack, and they ache when there's rain coming. I'm not as spry as I once was." Her eyes glittered. "But let's not even get into how good my hearing is. I am, however, an insomniac. So I repeat: something you boys want to tell me?" Her lips twitched.

Jamie snorted. "We are *so* busted."

Grandma chuckled. "Yes, you are. Now would you mind telling me how long this has been going on for?"

"Not that long." Stephen wasn't about to admit they'd been a couple less than a week. He didn't think she'd approve of them jumping into bed *that* fast. He was still reeling from the fact that she was taking it so well.

"And is it serious?"

Stephen glanced across the table at Jamie. "I'm happy for the first time in my life." Jamie's face glowed, and the light in his eyes made Stephen warm inside.

Grandma sighed. "I'll take that as a yes."

"All he needed was me in his life," Jamie said with a smile, his gaze locked on Stephen.

"You know it."

"Do your parents know?"

Stephen shook his head. "That's next. This week is to give us some breathing space before we tell them."

"A sort of honeymoon without a wedding," Jamie added. He gave her a keen glance. "You're taking this very well."

"Which part? Stephen having a male partner? Oh, I knew that was coming. As for what I heard last night, we're not going to discuss it." She coughed. "Although I might suggest one of you employs a gag in the future, if the... urge takes you in the middle of the night."

Stephen was pretty sure his jaw broke when it hit the floor. "Grandma?"

She gave him a frank stare. "You haven't seen my neighbors, Ed and Roy, have you? Trust me, if you had, you wouldn't be in the slightest bit surprised that I know about such things. Of course, if that kind of… activity interests you, you really should have planned your trip better." She smiled. "The leather masked ball isn't till next month."

Silence fell for a moment, broken by Jamie's loud guffaw. "*Now* I know who you remind me of. Betty White."

She beamed. "I'm going to take that as a compliment. Now, back to your parents… do you think you'll run into any resistance?"

"Not from my side," Jamie said, his expression growing more sober.

Stephen didn't blame him for his reaction. "I don't think my parents will be overjoyed."

Grandma shrugged. "You're not telling me anything I didn't expect. I should know my own daughter, after all. But they *should* be overjoyed." She finished her coffee. "Now, what are your plans for today?"

"Laze by the pool?" Jamie suggested. "Read? Swim?"

Stephen thought they all sounded great. Having watched Jamie swim the previous day, he was once again in awe of his boyfriend. Jamie lived his life to the full.

And if he can face life like that, with all it's thrown at him, then so can I.

"Unfortunately, I won't be around much today," Grandma said as she collected the breakfast dishes. "I *was* going to spend the day with you, but a friend called. He wants to go to the Harvest Festival, and I agreed to accompany him. I'm afraid I won't be back until dinner time this evening." She peered through the window at the back yard. "Pity. It's going to be a lovely day for sunbathing." Then she caught Stephen's gaze. "I do love my garden. Not only for its flower beds and the pool, but because it's so pleasant not to be overlooked by neighbors. Don't you agree?" Grandma gestured to the dishwasher. "Could you fill that, please, before you go out to the pool? Thank you." And with that, she left the kitchen.

Jamie stared after her, his mouth open. "I fucking *love* your grandma."

"Language, please," Grandma hollered from her room. "I know where the soap is."

Stephen chuckled. "She was right about her hearing."

"She's giving us the house to ourselves. And she as good as told us we could skinny dip in the pool, because no one can see in."

Stephen wasn't thinking about swimming. He was thinking about lying naked on a towel, the sun warming him all over, and Jamie beside him.

"Did you bring sunscreen?" Jamie asked as he went over to the countertop to fill the dishwasher.

"Yup. I'll go grab it, along with our towels." Stephen walked up behind him and bent down to whisper, "I'll bring the lube too."

The hitch in Jamie's breathing was delicious. Then he said quietly, "The Viagra is in my toiletries bag. I can only take it once a day, so make a decision—this afternoon or tonight?"

It took Stephen less than two seconds to decide. "I'll grab that too. Two tablets, right?"

Jamie chuckled. "Like I always say, you're a

fast learner."

Stephen kissed his neck, loving the shiver that coursed through him. "And tonight, I'll be inside you."

Another shiver, only this one was more pronounced. "Trust me, if everything worked the way it's supposed to, I'd be hard as a rock right now."

"That's why I'm bringing the Viagra. I want you hard in about an hour." Then he heard Grandma bustling about in her room. "Providing she's gone by then."

The last thing they wanted was an audience.

The sun was hot on his back, and sweat dripped off him onto Jamie's chest as he lay beneath Stephen on a towel. Jamie's face and neck were flushed, and the tide of red was spreading lower. His hands were on Stephen's thighs, stroking them as Stephen crouched over him, impaling himself again and again on Jamie's dick.

And fuck, it felt good.

"I could do this all day," he murmured, slowly sinking down onto Jamie's rigid shaft.

"And how long do you think we've been at it?" Jamie whispered. Then he caught his breath as Stephen quickened the pace. "Oh Lord, yes. Like that. God bless Viagra."

"Amen to that." Stephen was doing all the work,

but it was worth it to see how goddamn gorgeous Jamie looked as he lay there, Stephen's shadow falling over him.

"Does it feel different? Without the condom, I mean?" When Stephen nodded, Jamie smiled. "A good different?"

"I love the feeling that there's nothing between us," Stephen admitted. It had to be one of the quickest decisions they'd come to, and one he didn't regret. Getting tested together was all part of intimacy.

Jamie's breathing was shallow, his gaze locked on Stephen's face. "Wanna know what the best bits about this are?" he said hoarsely. "Because they're not what you might think."

"Tell me."

"Watching your face when I'm inside you. Seeing your reaction each time you bottom out, and I'm all the way in. Hearing the noises you make, those little whimpers when you're full of me." He smiled. "Watching your cock bob up and down stiffly, because it's so hard." His smile morphed into a grin. "Then there's the thrill of it all, not knowing if Ed or Roy next door will choose that moment to poke their heads above the fence to ask if they can borrow some Crisco or leather cleaner." His eyes twinkled.

Stephen laughed, and it pushed Jamie out of him. Jamie hurriedly guided his dick back to where it belonged, then rested his hands on Stephen's thighs. "I think I'm about to melt into a puddle of sweat or spunk—I'm not sure which at this point."

Stephen placed his knees on either side of Jamie's body, and began to rock back and forth, gaining momentum. "Can't take much more." He bent over Jamie to kiss him.

"Then come," Jamie begged. "Come on me. Let me feel it."

Stephen straightened, his fingers curled around his shaft as he tugged it, balls tingling as he neared completion. He gave a low cry as he shot hard, his spunk pulsing out to hit Jamie square in the middle of his chest. Jamie groaned, pulling him down into a fervent kiss, his arms locked around Stephen's neck. Stephen kissed his neck, his cheeks, his lips, his body shaking with each jolt of pleasure that arced through him.

Jamie brushed the hair back from his forehead. "You're soaked."

Stephen chuckled. "And you're surprised?" He frowned. "But you haven't—"

Jamie stopped his words. "I don't always, okay? But that doesn't mean it wasn't amazing. Because it was."

Whatever else he was about to say was lost in a series of low moans and cries that emanated from the neighboring yard. Stephen gaped at him, and Jamie covered his mouth as he attempted to smother his laughter. They remained frozen to the spot as the sounds died away.

"Not going to embarrass you further by sticking our heads above the fence," said a gruff voice at last, "but thank you. That was fucking hot."

"You could've *said* something," Stephen retorted. "You know, to let us know we weren't alone out here?"

"What, and spoil the fun?" A rough chuckle

rumbled out. "That was the best live porn show ever."

"And don't worry. We won't tell May what you were doing," said another voice. "By the way… that Crisco or leather cleaner comment? Fucking hilarious." Then they caught the sound of a door closing.

"The least they could've done is give us a round of applause," Jamie said, pouting.

That was all it took to have Stephen erupt into laughter again. Jamie slid out of him, and Stephen lay on top of him, sharing long, languorous kisses, their bodies slippery with sweat.

Stephen couldn't stop looking at him. "There's always a glow about you after sex," he remarked.

Jamie snickered. "That's not a glow—that's sunburn."

"Hey, I'm paying you a compliment. I'm telling you how much I love seeing that well-fucked look on you."

"Ditto." Jamie peered at the top of his head and chuckled. "I love the way your hair sticks up. It's cute." He slid his hands down Stephen's back. "I love the feel of your skin, slick with sweat. I love how you look at me, as if you can't believe I'm here, that we just made love."

"I love you," Stephen said softly. "Every bit of you. Even the bits that don't work." And now that he'd finally said the words, he knew he'd picked the right time.

Jamie swallowed, and tears glistened as they spilled onto his cheeks. "Love you too." He wiped his eyes. "You have no idea how long I've been waiting to hear you say that."

Stephen kissed him, long and slow, and Jamie sighed into it. When they parted, Stephen stroked Jamie's shock of hair. "Sorry I made you wait."

Jamie inclined his head toward the fence. "Thanks for waiting till they went indoors to say that."

He smiled. "I think it might have earned us a standing ovation. But that was just for you. Next week I get to tell my family that I love you."

"Don't." Jamie stopped him with a kiss. "Don't let's talk about going home. I want to savor every moment of this week, so let's not spoil it. Home means work and routine and deadlines, and I don't want to think about *any* of that."

"Okay. One thing before I change the subject, and we have a swim?" Stephen kissed him again, drinking in the smell of him. "When we get back, I'm not looking for a house anymore." Another lingering kiss, but this time he pressed his lips to Jamie's chest. "I've already found my home."

K.C. Wells

Chapter Twenty-Four

Jamie loved it when they lay like this in bed, each end of one pillow between their knees as they faced each other, connected by it. He knew before sleep took them, Stephen would close the gap, inching forward until their bodies touched, and they'd fall asleep with Stephen's arm draped over his waist.

"So who do we tell first—your parents or mine?" Stephen asked, leisurely stroking Jamie's chest. Jamie loved the constant touches, the soft caresses, the reminders of their connection.

"I've been thinking about that." Jamie cupped Stephen's nape and pulled him into a kiss. He closed his eyes and enjoyed the feel of Stephen's mouth on his, the gentle hand that curved around his neck, the soft sigh of contentment that escaped Stephen's lips.

Stephen broke the kiss and pulled back to look him in the eye. "Was that a soften-the-blow kiss?"

He smiled. "It was more of a I-haven't-kissed-you-in-five-minutes-so-I-need-to-do-it-now kiss. And as for the parents, I have a plan."

Stephen groaned. "Oh God. Do I want to hear this?" Jamie landed a soft punch in his belly. "Hey!"

"Listen to it at least." Jamie kissed his fingertips and pressed them lightly to Stephen's torso. "And I'm sorry."

"I'll live. Now tell me your plan."

"How about we throw a party? And we invite

your parents, my parents, Liz, Phil…" Jamie grinned. "A small, intimate gathering. Party food, alcohol, whatever. Then we make an announcement. Think of it as a not-an-engagement party."

Stephen arched his eyebrows. "Why do it that way?"

"We'd be stacking the odds in our favor. My folks will be behind us, because hey, they already love you like their own son. We know Liz will have our backs, because *duh*, I've got heel marks there where she kept kicking me to make a move on you. And Phil seems like an okay guy. So that's four people rooting for us."

Stephen nodded slowly. "And my parents would be less inclined to say something negative and look like assholes. Not that they *are* assholes, you understand."

"No, they're not," Jamie agreed. "They look at me and see obstacles, that's all."

"Like I did?"

Jamie cupped Stephen's cheek. "You're a faster learner than they are. Think about it. My parents have had eight years to learn not to underestimate me. How long have your parents had? Hmm?"

"You know they're going to say we're moving too fast. After all, I only moved back here last month."

Jamie sighed. "Listen to me, my sweet, glass-half-empty guy. We've been building up to this most of our lives. Meeting again was meant to be." He traced the line of Stephen's jaw with his fingers. "You're the other half of me."

Stephen's soft *oh* made his heart sing.

"And besides, we're telling them we're a

couple, not announcing that we're getting married next week."

He smiled. "Okay, I like the plan."

Jamie beamed. "Great. We can talk about it tomorrow."

"Why not now?" Stephen sighed. "You're tired."

"Not really."

He loved the way Stephen's eyes lit up. "Oh? Oh!"

Jamie chuckled. "Yeah, I'm rethinking that whole 'fast learner' comment."

"What can I do to make up for my slowness?" Stephen's hand was already on Jamie's dick, giving it casual tugs.

"You can grab the wedge, for starters."

Fuck, the look on Stephen's face was *so* gratifying....

Jamie took one last look around the living room. Everywhere was neat and tidy, because hey, Stephen's mom could spot a cobweb from fifty feet away. The food was ready in the kitchen, and glasses stood on the coffee table.

The champagne was in the refrigerator.

"I think we're ready," he called out to Stephen who was in the bathroom.

"We'd better be. They're on their way. Mom messaged me."

Liz had already messaged Jamie. She and Phil were arriving with his parents.

"You know what I really want from tonight?" Jamie mused. "For your parents to see how *normal* this place is. That you're living in an ordinary house, not one full of contraptions to make my life easier."

Stephen walked into the living room, looking smart in black jeans and a pale blue button-down shirt. "I thought that was my job? Not that you need me."

"Come here," Jamie said softly. He pulled Stephen down into a lingering kiss. When he was done, he gazed into Stephen's eyes. "I will *always* need you, okay?"

Stephen swallowed. "Ditto." He stiffened. "I hear a car." He tried to straighten, but Jamie laughed and pulled him down for one more kiss.

"Okay. *Now* you can let them in."

His parents were the first to arrive, and once the hugging was done, he got Stephen to pour them all a drink. Mom took Jamie aside, and crouched beside his chair.

"Okay. Why the party?"

Jamie gave her as innocent a look as he could muster. "We felt like throwing one, that's all."

Mom arched her eyebrows at that, but said nothing. She got up and glanced at the walls. "You've put up your sketches."

"Yeah, most of them." There was no way anyone was seeing their bedroom. "It was Stephen's idea."

"If you ever decide to give up web design, you'd have a great career as an artist." She grinned. "I kept your first ever painting, you know."

"You did?" Jamie couldn't think back that far. "What did I paint?"

She smiled. "Stephen. You did it in kindergarten. I had it on the refrigerator for months."

He gaped at her. "Tell me you've got it someplace safe."

Mom nodded. "It's with all your other masterpieces in a box in the attic."

He guffawed. "Masterpieces."

Mom squeezed his shoulder. "They are to me."

The doorbell rang. "And here come the rest of the guests." His heartbeat sped up a little. "I'd better go welcome them." He left Mom in the living room and wheeled himself to the front door, taking in a deep breath.

Here we go.

Stephen's belly had been full of butterflies all evening. He could tell from the glances passed between his parents that they knew something was up. Not that they said anything.

And speaking of saying something…

He went into the kitchen where Jamie was removing a tray of hot snacks from the oven. "When do you think we should make the announcement?"

Jamie grinned. "Let me put these out first, okay?"

Stephen grabbed an oven glove and took the

tray from him. "They're all chatting away in there. Our moms are reminiscing, by the sound of it."

"Of course. They've got eight years of catching up to do."

Stephen was glad they'd decided to throw a party. It was about time the two families reconnected. He tipped the snacks onto a serving dish, his stomach in knots.

Jamie laid a hand on his arm. "It's going to be fine. You wait and see."

All Stephen wanted to do in that moment was kiss him. "I love your optimism." He lowered his voice. "Almost as much as I love you."

"Then let's go share the good news. And Stephen?" Jamie's eyes were warm. "I love you too."

There was no way Stephen wasn't going to kiss him after that. He pressed his lips to Jamie's, drinking in Jamie's familiar smell. Then he straightened. "Showtime."

Jamie led the way into the living room, Stephen behind him. He deposited the dish on the coffee table. "More nibbles. I thought I heard Phil's stomach rumbling from the kitchen."

Phil snickered. "Wasn't me," he said with a sideways glance at Liz.

"Hey!" She whacked him on the arm.

Jamie cleared his throat. "Can we have your attention, please?"

All eyes turned toward him, and Jamie gave Stephen a meaningful stare. Stephen didn't need to be a mind reader to know that look said, 'Get your ass over here.' He joined Jamie, standing beside him.

"Now, I know you've been wondering why we

threw this little soiree," Jamie began.

"Well, I didn't see any skeletons or zombies out on the front lawn, or giant spiders climbing over the house so I'm guessing it's not an early Halloween party," his dad joked.

Jamie jerked his head toward Stephen, his eyes bright, lips parted. Stephen shook his head. "No. No zombies. No spiders either."

Jamie did his familiar pout. "Spoilsport." Stephen coughed and nudged his arm. "Oh yeah. So... we've asked you here because we have something to celebrate."

Liz grinned. "Oh really. I can't think what *that* could be." Stephen fired her a warning glance.

"Stephen's been sharing this house for a while now, while he was saving up for a place of his own. Well, he's given up that idea." Jamie gazed up at him with such a look of naked adoration that Stephen's heart soared. "Seeing as he's going to be living here permanently."

Stephen smiled. "With my boyfriend." Then he bent down to kiss Jamie on the lips.

Liz's squeal broke the silence. "About time!" She dashed over to them and threw her arms around Jamie. "Congrats, bro." Phil came too, his hand extended to shake Stephen's. Maureen and David came over, their eyes shining, both smiling broadly.

Stephen glanced at his parents, who stood there with open mouths and dazed looks. Stephen went over to them, still smiling. "Mom, Dad? I've never been happier."

Dad cleared his throat. "And *I'm* happy to hear that." He glanced at Jamie. "Are you sure you know what you're taking on?" he said in a low voice. Mom nudged him, and he frowned. "Well, you've got to be thinking the same thing too."

Mom sighed. "I'm glad you and Jamie are together, really I am. It's sort of fitting, when you think about it. But..." She gazed across the room at Jamie.

Maureen joined them. "When Jamie had his accident," she said quietly, "we all went through a period of adjustment. At first, we thought our hopes and dreams for his future were shattered. Then we were just happy to have him alive. As time went on, we did our best to encourage him, to tell him to push for what he wanted. And he *did* that, over and over again. The only thing he didn't succeed at, was finding someone to love him."

"We watched him go through heartache after heartache," David added, joining them. "And all the time we kept praying for someone to come along who would see the miracle that was our son. Who would see the man with a huge capacity for love. Someone who would love him the way he deserved to be loved." He smiled. "What we didn't realize was that Jamie had already met him."

Mom's eyes glistened. "I love that they found each other again. I ... All I want is for Stephen to have... a full life."

Stephen stared at her as comprehension dawned. "But I *do*, Mom." He chuckled. "You need to believe me on that score. And if you need more convincing, talk to Grandma."

Mom blinked. "I see."

Jamie wheeled over to them. "Am I missing out

on something?"

Stephen laughed and took his hand. *Later*, he mouthed.

"Hey, don't we get to toast the happy couple, or something?" Liz called out.

Jamie squeezed his hand. "I'll get the champagne." He headed for the kitchen.

Mom gave him a hug. "I'm happy for you," she whispered.

"Thanks." He kissed her cheek.

Dad shook his hand. "If you had to fall in love with someone, I guess there isn't anyone better than your best friend."

"So who's gonna get to the altar first? You two, or me and Phil?" Liz asked.

Stephen loved Phil's incredulous stare and hard swallow.

"I didn't know it was a race," Jamie teased as he entered the room, the bottle of champagne placed carefully in his lap. "Anyhow, we're not engaged." He squinted at Stephen. "Unless you're about to get down on one knee and pull a ring out of your... pocket." His eyes gleamed.

Stephen laughed. "I hadn't planned on it." And besides, that would probably have been a bit too far out of his parents' comfort zone. He took the bottle and opened it, popping the cork as gently as he could. When all the glasses were filled, everyone took one.

Maureen raised her glass. "To Jamie and Stephen. May their lives be filled with sunshine."

Stephen clinked Jamie's glass. "I'll drink to that."

Epilogue

The following summer

"Oh, man, that was awesome!" Jamie said as he dried himself off with a towel. "Did you see?"

"I didn't take my eyes off you." Stephen pressed a hand to his chest. "I was having palpitations watching you bounce over the water."

Jamie laughed. It had been his third session on an adaptive water ski, and all he wanted to do was get out there again. The exhilaration he'd experienced, holding onto the bar and skimming through the waves...

"You should try it," he suggested. "We could go out together."

Stephen snorted. "I'm not that brave. I'll leave the daredevilry to you."

Jamie laughed. "You said that about skiing, and you were fantastic on the slopes." He couldn't resist. "Next stop—paragliding!"

Stephen shook his head slowly. "No. No. No. End of conversation. Talk Phil into it, by all means. He's already said he'd love to do that." He speared Jamie with a hard stare. "And no, Jamie, 'I dare ya' will *not* work this time."

Damn.

"Who was that guy you were talking to, when you came in?" Stephen asked.

Jamie grinned. "That was the best part. He's a

champion disabled sit down wakeboarder. He said he does jumps and all kinds of tricks."

"Wakeboarding?"

He nodded. "You ride the wakes on a board, except in his case, there's a special seat on it that he's strapped into." Jamie figured he'd wait until later to spring it on Stephen that the guy had offered to let him try. "He was a skateboarder until he had an accident. Now he's a paraplegic too." He glanced down at his damp shorts. They'd dry off soon enough in the heat. "Where's Marie?"

"She's waiting for us at the beach. Declan wants to build a sandcastle with Uncle Jamie. Then Natasha wants to bury you in the sand and make you into a merman."

He laughed. "I can't help it if your nephew and niece love me." They were great kids, and he loved taking them off Marie's hands when she was busy with the baby. Not that he didn't enjoy sitting in the rocking chair with baby Owen too.

"She asked me again this morning if we'd thought any more about her offer."

Jamie pulled on a dry T-shirt. "And what did you tell her?"

"What we discussed last night. I thanked her for offering to be our surrogate, and told her we really appreciated it, but that we couldn't see ourselves doing that when there are so many kids who need to be adopted."

Jamie nodded. When Marie had sat them down and come out with the proposal, he'd been blown away by her generosity. Greg was keen on the idea too. But Jamie and Stephen had talked it through, long

into the night. They both wanted kids, that much was obvious, but the idea of adoption made more sense. "Besides, she said Owen's birth had been rough on her." Selfless as the offer was, they
wouldn't let her go through another pregnancy just for them.

Stephen chuckled. "Then I told her we already had our hands full with Lou and Bud."

Jamie rolled his eyes. "If parenthood is anything like looking after two hyperactive dachshunds, we're gonna be exhausted."

Stephen laughed. "I spoke with your mom this morning. She's pretty much exhausted already, and she's only had them four days."

He wheeled along the jetty, heading for where Stephen had parked the rental car. Their first visit to Carmel had been perfect so far. Jamie could see why Stephen had loved the climate. This was their last evening before they left for San Diego.

Jamie hoped he was doing the right thing.

"I think you'll make a wonderful father," Stephen said as they neared the car. "But maybe we should look into it seriously when we get home? Maybe sign us up with some adoption agencies?" He huffed. "Who are probably going to want us to jump through several hundred hoops before we get even close to adopting a kid."

Jamie had been thinking about that too. "And what if the powers that be would be happier if we had a piece of paper?"

Stephen smiled as he unlocked the car. "Then I'll get down on one knee and pull a ring out of my… pocket." His eyes twinkled. "I wouldn't mind getting married. Would you?"

Jamie shrugged as he lifted his legs into the car. "Maybe one day. Not sure I'm ready yet." He kept his tone neutral, even though his heartbeat sped up a little. He glanced across at Stephen, in time to see him straighten his features.

Aha.

Stephen said nothing as he folded the chair and placed it in the trunk.

Jamie watched him as he got into the car. "You okay?"

"Yeah, I'm fine." Stephen switched on the engine. "Let's go build a sandcastle."

Jamie reached over and stroked his thigh. "Love you."

Stephen lifted Jamie's hand to his lips and kissed it. "Love you too." He pulled out of the parking lot, and they headed along the coast road to the beach Marie and the kids usually frequented.

"You still okay with our trip to San Diego tomorrow?"

"Sure."

Jamie glanced at him. "You don't *sound* so sure."

Stephen shrugged. "I guess I'm not clear on why you want us to go there, that's all."

"I told you. I wanna see where you grew up. Your high school, the beach you played on, the house you lived in…"

"And that's the only reason?"

Jamie sighed. "Plus, I think it's time we exorcised a few… ghosts."

"Aha. *Now* we're getting somewhere." Stephen

kept his eyes on the road ahead. "You really think we need to do this?"

"Yes, I do. And I'm asking you to trust me on this." His heart was pounding. *Come on, Stephen. Trust me.*

There was a pause, but finally Stephen nodded. "Okay. We're going to San Diego." Then he chuckled. "Well, you've already bought the plane tickets and booked us into a hotel, so we might as well."

Jamie squeezed Stephen's hand. "Thank you," he said sincerely.

Please, Lord, let this go the way I hope?

"It's been wonderful having you two stay with us." Marie poured Stephen another cup of coffee. "Only, stay longer next time?"

"We will, I promise." He leaned back in his chair, watching Jamie and Natasha battle it out on her PlayStation. By the look of things, Jamie was winning.

"Back to work next week, then? I'm sure Dad will be pleased."

Stephen nodded. "He says there's a pile of folders on my desk."

"Is Jamie still doing his web design?" Greg asked.

"Yes, but he's got something else on the go at

the moment. And it's a little… different." That was putting it mildly.

"Do tell." Marie's eyes gleamed.

"It's sort of an artistic project." Stephen glanced toward the couch where Natasha was sitting with Jamie, then lowered his voice. "He's writing a guide to sex positions for people with disabilities."

"Seriously?" Marie widened her eyes.

"Yup. He's doing all the illustrations."

Marie darted a glance in Jamie's direction. "Then he's apparently worked hard on his drawing skills since he was a kid. If I recall, he had to have something in front of him to be able to draw it."

Stephen nodded. "He still has poor visual memory."

"Then how is he—*who* is he drawing?"

Stephen groaned. "One wall of our bedroom is covered in photos—of us. He set up a camera, and then we… got to it." He was sure his cheeks were scarlet.

Greg let out a gasp. "Just how graphic are these illustrations?"

Jamie chose that moment to look over his shoulder and grin at him, then went back to his game.

Stephen chuckled. "Don't ask. I think he only gets away with some of them because they're pencil drawings."

"And it's going to be published?" Marie asked.

He nodded. "It'll be out next year, so they tell us."

She grinned. "I'll make sure to reserve myself a copy."

He stared at her, aghast. "Why would you do

that?"

"I want to be able to show everyone I meet. I'll say, look what my brother's partner did." She was still grinning.

"She's yanking your chain," Greg informed him. "She's probably going to give it to some friends of ours. One of them is a paraplegic." He gave her a hard stare. "Because I'm *certain* she wouldn't be looking at it just to see what her brother's partner looks like naked, right?"

"Oh, absolutely not." She gazed back at Greg with an innocent look in her eyes.

Stephen shook his head. "It's amazing. You and Liz could be sisters."

What were the odds?

"How long will you be spending in San Diego?" Marie asked.

"A few days. Enough to show Jamie my old haunts." And that was exactly what they were.

Marie glanced at Jamie, then reached out for Stephen's hand. "You're not the same man you were when you lived out here."

"I'm not?"

She smiled. "Being with Jamie has changed you."

"I needed changing, huh?" Not that she was wrong. Even he could see it. Jamie had brought light to his life.

"You look at things differently now, that's all. It's like you see the positive in situations, whereas before…"

"Yeah, I know." Stephen smiled. "It's hard to be negative when you live with someone like Jamie."

Thank God for the impulse to indulge in nostalgia. If he hadn't gone to Horn Pond that day...

He gazed at the back of Jamie's head. Seconds later, Jamie turned to meet his gaze.

Love you, Stephen mouthed.

Love you too.

Stephen paused at the threshold. "Tell me again why we're here?" He hadn't set foot in that particular San Diego gay bar for over a year, and he wasn't sure he wanted to go in now. It didn't hold good memories for him.

Jamie took his hand. "We're here because you told me about this place—eventually—and I wanted to see it for myself. Besides, this time you're walking in there for a drink, not looking to find a date. Okay?" He smiled. "Because you've already got a date. Me."

He laughed at that. "Let's get in there. I wonder if it's changed much." He pushed open the door and held it for Jamie, then followed him in. The music was as loud as ever, the lights as bright and colorful. Men stood around drinking and talking, and a lot of gazes instantly swept in their direction, aimed at Jamie's chair. Then the guys went back to their drinks and conversations.

"There's a table over there," Jamie said, pointing to one on the edge of the dance floor. "I'll go grab it, while you get us a drink."

Stephen went up to the bar and ordered two

drinks. One glance at the bar's patrons revealed no one he recognized—at least, no one who'd caused him distress in the past—and for that he was grateful. But he saw many men who'd been frequent visitors. They were clearly doing the same thing they'd always done.

They were on the lookout to find someone who'd make a difference in their lives.

He took the drinks over to where Jamie sat, then joined him, watching the proceedings. A couple of times he glimpsed an expression he knew only too well. That look of longing, searching, hoping...

"That's not you anymore," Jamie said above the music.

Stephen jerked his head toward him. "How did you know...?"

"That's why I brought you here." He gestured to some of the men surrounding them. "You were like them once. Look at their faces. Can you see yourself in them?"

He nodded. "I was thinking the same thing when I was at the bar."

"But like I said, that's not you. What makes you different?"

Stephen considered the question. "Maybe it's that I found what I was looking for."

"Do you still think you're a loser?"

Stephen smiled. "No. Not anymore. I have a good life. A good job. A home. An extended family who adores me." He met Jamie's gaze. "A partner who loves me."

Jamie nodded. "And if you'll have him... a husband."

Stephen stared at the small black box Jamie removed from his jeans pocket, his heartbeat racing. "I... I thought you weren't ready to get married."

Jamie grinned. "I lied. In fact, to prove how big a liar I am? I bought this in Boston and brought it with me, to propose right here. Of course, I can't get down on one knee, but it's the thought that counts." He gave Stephen a meaningful stare. "Well? Do I have an answer?"

Stephen blinked. "You haven't asked the question yet."

Jamie narrowed his gaze briefly. "Fine. Stephen Taylor, will you marry me?"

Around them, some of the guys fell silent, their attention focused on Stephen and Jamie.

Stephen folded his arms. "I don't know. I haven't seen the ring yet." That caused a ripple of chuckles.

Jamie rolled his eyes, but opened the box. "There. Satisfied? And before you ask, bean pole, it *will* fit."

"Oh well, in that case, yes, I'll marry you."

Jamie raised his eyes heavenward as the applause broke out. "Hallelujah!"

"Hey, tall dude. Did you two just get engaged?" the bartender hollered. More guys were crowding around them, but Stephen only had eyes for Jamie.

"Yeah, we did." Stephen got up from his chair, walked around the table, bent down, and kissed Jamie on the lips, amid more applause from those around them. Then he gazed into Jamie's eyes. "Do you know how happy I am right now?"

Jamie beamed. "Then I did what I set out to do."

"That was your goal—to marry me?"

He laughed. "No, bean pole. Marrying you is the icing on the cake." He locked gazes with Stephen. "I *do* get it, you know. You've spent most of your life seeing only the problems that lie in wait for you, lurking in the shadows." He smiled. "My goal was to get you to see past the shadows and look into the light. Because that's where I've been waiting for you."

Stephen stared at him. "That sounds almost poetic. Did you just think of all that?"

Jamie shook his head. "It's all I've thought about since you walked back into my life."

Stephen kissed him again. "You know what? I like it here in the light. I think I'll move here permanently."

"What—to this bar?" Jamie teased.

Stephen rolled his eyes. "*Duh*. I'm going to finish my drink, and then we're going back to our hotel. And forget about sightseeing and me reminiscing about living here. We are *not* going to leave our hotel room until it's time to take a taxi to the airport."

Jamie grinned. "However shall we pass the time?"

Stephen laughed. "You're a smart guy. You'll think of something."

Jamie bit his lip. "There *was* something I've been wanting to do for a while."

"And what's that?" Stephen was sure his voice had never sounded so husky.

"Well, there's a whole series of wheelchair sex positions I've been meaning to draw for the book." Jamie's eyes sparkled. "Think how many we could work on while we're in that hotel room."

"Haven't we done that already?"

Jamie widened his eyes. "Dude, we've barely scratched the surface."

Suddenly Stephen stilled. "Wait—you brought your sketchpad and pencils with you?" He narrowed his gaze. "You were going to do this anyway."

Jamie grinned. "Oops. Busted."

"Then what are we waiting for?" Stephen got out his phone. "Which do you think will get here first—cab, Uber or Lyft?"

The End

About the Author

K.C. Wells lives on an island off the south coast of the UK, surrounded by natural beauty. She writes about men who love men, and can't even contemplate a life that doesn't include writing.

The rainbow rose tattoo on her back with the words 'Love is Love' and 'Love Wins' is her way of hoisting a flag. She plans to be writing about men in love - be it sweet and slow, hot or kinky - for a long while to come.

K.C. Wells

Other titles by K.C. Wells

Learning to Love
Michael & Sean
Evan & Daniel
Josh & Chris
Final Exam

Sensual Bonds
A Bond of Three
A Bond of Truth

Merrychurch Mysteries
Truth Will Out
Roots of Evil
A Novel Murder

Love, Unexpected
Debt
Burden

Dreamspun Desires
The Senator's Secret
Out of the Shadows
My Fair Brady
Under the Covers

Lions & Tigers & Bears
A Growl, a Roar, and a Purr

A Snarl, a Splash, and a Shock

Love Lessons Learned
First
Waiting for You
Step by Step
Bromantically Yours
BFF

Collars & Cuffs
An Unlocked Heart
Trusting Thomas
Someone to Keep Me (K.C. Wells & Parker Williams)
A Dance with Domination
Damian's Discipline (K.C. Wells & Parker Williams)
Make Me Soar
Dom of Ages (K.C. Wells & Parker Williams)
Endings and Beginnings (K.C. Wells & Parker Williams)

Secrets – with Parker Williams
Before You Break
An Unlocked Mind
Threepeat
On the Same Page

Wrangled

Second Sight
In His Sights
In Plain Sight

CrossBow Protection
Broken Warrior

Standalones
Kel's Keeper
Here For You
Sexting The Boss
Gay on a Train
Sunshine & Shadows
Double or Nothing
Back from the Edge
Switching it up
Out for You (FREE)
State of Mind (FREE)
No More Waiting (FREE)
Watch and Learn
My Best Friend's Brother
Princely Submission
Bears in the Woods
Holy Hell – with Parker Williams
Teasing Tim
Str8 B8

Anthologies

<u>Fifty Gays of Shade</u>
Winning Will's Heart

<u>Come, Play</u>
Watch and Learn

<u>Writing as Tantalus</u>
Damon & Pete: Playing with Fire